Praises For:

A Single Day of Peace

A Single Day of Peace takes the reader on a fictional journey between two seemingly opposite worlds: the corporate business landscape of New York City and the austere Catholic Church. The protagonist demonstrates how the values and qualities needed to live a meaningful life do not come from the rules and social norms instilled by either world but rather from 50 guiding principles the author clearly lays out. The unique methodology of using a fictional storyline to provide self-help to the reader will appeal to readers young and old.

— **Lexi Marie,** Bookstagrammer @completely__booked.

***

I have known Stephen for years and his spiritual principles shine through in all he does. Now in his book, he shares the philosophies that have guided him. In an age where many of us are questioning our religion, our faith, and our purpose, it is paramount we reconnect with our spirituality. Stephen's book will help you do just that—and you will be a better person because of it.

—**Tracy Byrnes,** financial advisor, former financial journalist/TV anchor and forever seeker of that day of peace.

***

This novel needs to be made into a movie! Matt Damon would kill the scenes as a Catholic Priest on a mission to revive faith. The appearances with *Jimmy Fallon* and on *60 Minutes* transcend entertainment. While I am a Latter-day Saint, I promised Stephen I'd withhold my theological views and simply put on my "editor" hat. That said, *A SINGLE DAY OF PEACE* would make an inspiring and entertaining movie.

— **Rick Bennett,** former one-man ad agency for *ORACLE* and *Salesforce.com*

I read about 50 books a year, and this was one of the best in a long time. I was so engaged in the story, that I had to keep reminding myself that it was a fictional story. Many religious denominations would benefit from the book's suggestions. Stephen's book will leave you feeling positive, inspired, uplifted, and ready to take on the world.

—**Luanne Thibault,** Book Aficionado and editor.

***

A thought provoking and inspiring read on spirituality. Balancing a new perspective on traditional Catholic tenets with practical business acumen. A Single Day of Peace brings you much more than peace, but a tranquil harmony between spirituality and business purpose.

—**Allison Pagni,** software executive.

***

I'm not a particularly religious person and I feel this book hits the issues of the church perfectly. The controversial topics keep you fixated. It provided me with a desire to look inside myself to create a more fulfilling and successful life. The book's message and guidance will resonate very well with my peers.

—**Matt Mancino,** technology leader.

A SINGLE DAY OF PEACE

*An Inspirational Novel Revealing 50 Principles
That Can Transform Your Life*

STEPHEN D'ANGELO

Published by KHARIS PUBLISHING, imprint of KHARIS MEDIA LLC.

Copyright © 2021 Stephen D'Angelo

ISBN-13: 978-1-63746-033-7

ISBN-10: 1-63746-033-3

Library of Congress Control Number:2021936364

All KHARIS PUBLISHING products are available at special quantity discounts for bulk purchase for sales promotions, premiums, fund-raising, and educational needs. For details, contact:

Kharis Media LLC
Tel: 1-479-599-8657
support@kharispublishing.com
www.kharispublishing.com

Disclaimer

Most of the characters, their actions, events, locations, and organizations in this book are fictitious and any resemblance to actual persons (living or dead), their actions, events, or locations is purely coincidental. Any of the companies, individuals, and locations in this book that are known are used fictitiously and do not represent that they have endorsed, participated in, or supported this story in any way. The use of the companies, individuals, and locations are simply part of the author's creativity in telling this story.

The advice and strategies found within may not be suitable for every situation. This work is sold with the understanding that neither the author nor the publisher can be held responsible for the results accrued from the advice in this book.

Through the power of God,
The energy of the universe,
and
The law of attraction,
Great things are possible.

CONTENTS

Preface

This book is for anyone who seeks self-improvement, growth, is navigating a spiritual journey, or pursuing self-actualization. If you seek greater fulfillment, happiness, peace, and success in your life, then this book is for you.

The larger purpose of *A Single Day of Peace* is to make the world a better place--one single day of peace at a time. Each of us has the opportunity to become more mentally and emotionally healthy and, when we do, our world becomes healthier, too. The opportunity and ability to create the world we want for ourselves is within our reach. Improving ourselves spiritually and emotionally allows us to have a dramatic, positive impact on others and, hence, make this world a better place for all. When you evolve as an individual, your energy touches those around you and they evolve.

My intent is not to promote any specific religious beliefs, but to intrigue those of many beliefs. If you believe there is a God, that there is one or many gods, see God as a universal energy, or believe in any Higher Power for that matter, this book will help you forge a deeper connection to your own spirituality.

The 50 success principles outlined in the final chapter can improve many aspects of your life. These principles embrace what I call spiritual leadership. This means guiding yourself and others with a positive spirit for constructive change. We all have the ability to lead, regardless of what we do. As parents, teachers, students, friends, husbands, wives, businesspeople, investors, athletes, etc., we have the opportunity and often the requirement to lead. The principles I offer in this book can help us succeed.

I use the Catholic Church as the setting for my message. My own spirituality derives from growing up Catholic and still enjoying the teachings of my Church. I believe in God, I believe in Jesus Christ, BUT I believe the Church can be more effective in teaching and inspiring the world. I suspect followers of many religions feel the same.

The ideas, recommendations, and inspirations provided throughout the book come from over 30 years of experience working as an executive, working with many who achieved success, coaching/mentoring executives, and interacting with people around the world. In my work as a business leader, I encountered many who brought strong principles and ethics to their endeavors and some who did not. I shared interactions with spiritual leaders, billionaires, and professional athletes. Over the course of years, I also had great mentors of my own. As part of my quest, I researched success, failure, motivation, wealth building, spirituality, leadership, meditation, and many other life-improving approaches.

I then took all this information and applied it to my life and saw the positive impact it had when I did things right ... and also the way things can go a bit sideways when I get lazy and don't apply these principles. I have been very lucky to have interacted with people from many walks of life, and to be blessed with the desire and ability to observe and learn from them all. I thank all of the people I have had a connection with over the years because, in some way, they all helped carve out what is *me*. It is that learning that I share with you. It is my hope that this story touches you in a way to see things differently and to evolve in a positive direction.

This book delivers its message by navigating the fictional journey of Mark Tossi, a business executive who becomes a Catholic priest. He integrates the principles of his business success with his spiritual teachings and acquires millions of inspired followers. Due to his unconventional approach and bold prediction as to what could happen to Jesus Christ if He returned, the church rejects Father Mark. He furthers his spiritual journey by traveling the Camino de Santiago pilgrimage route in Spain and documents 50 principles of success to help people live happier, more successful, and more fulfilled lives.

The heart of this story is about the universal search we all undertake to find our true spirit. Self-realization often requires courage to challenge the status quo and conventional beliefs in order to find and be who we are meant to be.

Chapter 17 presents the 50 principles of success and is structured in such a way that you can focus on one principle per day. Focusing on one principle each day becomes its own spiritual practice, and the means by which you can integrate these principles into your daily life.

I hope you enjoy the story as it provides inspiration and guidance on your life's journey. Thank you for every word you read.

CHAPTER 1

People often say to me, "Father Mark, I am so inspired by the way you love the Catholic Church." I'm honored by their compliment, so I smile and offer appreciation but, inside, uneasy emotions are the norm. I'm torn, frustrated, and discontented. Unfortunately, this seasick feeling began shortly after my ordination. Worse yet, it has been growing more intense with each passing day. I feel the seas getting rougher and rougher by the day.

As I think of my life before my priestly duties, my business success partly grew through transparent conversation, and my willingness to have the difficult discussions. That approach positively impacted everyone around me.

But that is not the way of institutionalized religion. Now, I'm disappointed in myself. I have kept all too quiet. I have suppressed the voice that wants to shake the essence of the Church.

People are starving for the Church to be renewed. We see how they suffer and need us to uplift their spirits. We recognize our precious parishioners leaving in droves. Where is our energy of compassion to guide our followers? Jesus fed 5,000 with so little, and we have so much within our reach to help and restore millions. Why aren't we doing better?

I knew the "how" of the Catholic Church would be very different from my former profession, but I didn't realize the apathy would be so great. The frequent unwillingness to call out the obvious issues we face, not to mention the crises of abuse scandals, appalls me. Some days it feels like a conspiracy with so few willing to talk about our ineptitude. Some do, some very brave few, but not enough. Aren't we supposed to be spiritual leaders? Aren't we supposed to be the bold ones that deal with society's problems head on? Aren't we supposed to protect the weak by being strong?

As a business leader, I always found it easy to address the elephant in the room. But that is not such an easy thing to do in the Church. I know my silence will not last. I fear it will break through like the bulls running in the streets of Pamplona.

The Lenten season is almost upon us. Will this holy time inspire us, inspire me to be transformed?

Seven weeks later

Father Mark Tossi lies in bed sleepless, staring at the barely lit ceiling. He turns his head slowly to the right to see the time on the nightstand digital clock. It is 3:02 a.m. Today is Easter. Tonight, like many nights, he can't sleep. Instead, he's haunted by a persistent realization that the Catholic society—actually, the Christian society—is not receiving the full benefit of what the Holy Spirit can provide. He ponders his own failure to transform how his congregation thinks and acts.

Father Mark Tossi is a 48-year-old enthusiastic priest and passionate believer in the power of Christianity. Ever since he can remember, spreading the idea of the power of God and even becoming a priest drew Father Mark toward preaching. When he was 13 and expressed his wish to his mother, she did not support this career choice. She worried that the perils of priesthood would be too difficult. Could her son endure the sacrifices and immense responsibilities? He came to the priesthood later in life by a circuitous route.

Mark's congregation is St. Jude Church in a small town in Ocean Crest, New Jersey. Set in a beach community, Father Mark's congregation grows in the summer but also enjoys a loyal local year-round following.

Father Mark falls back into a restless sleep only to be awakened by the thunderous sound of the singing of the Lord's Prayer. Was he dreaming? The clock now reads 4:46 a.m. He realizes that he was dreaming.

A few hours later, he finds himself in church celebrating the Easter liturgy. Until this moment, the day had been a bit of a sleepy blur.

There is standing-room-only in the church on this sunny and pleasant 58-degree day, one of those beach days when the breeze is just perfect. From a few blocks away, the sea scent wafts through the air. The large gathering is a magnificent sight on this most holy day. Father Mark's congregants tend to be upscale. Many reside in beautiful beach homes; for some these are their second homes. They are mostly professionals, investment bankers, software leaders, entrepreneurs, and finance experts.

Most have mastered the art of finance to purchase homes in their dream community. As in most upscale towns, some residents have stretched a bit beyond their means to live here. Children are everywhere. The churchgoers' attire is a blend of shorts, beach sandals, sundresses, golf shirts, and even a few Easter bonnets. Some of the elderly men are in suits; after all, it is Easter Sunday. Smiles abound. Colors are bright.

There is a long silence after the gospel reading. Father Mark is to give his homily. He hesitates. The two other priests serving Mass with him are close friends. Monsignor Joseph Byrne has been with St. Jude Church for 11 years and knows most of the year-round parishioners by their first names. Father Frank McCormick is from a parish in Newark, New Jersey and often visits St. Jude's to participate in mass. Monsignor Joseph and Father Frank met 19 years ago at a retreat. Both wonder why Father Mark hesitates.

The faithful in the congregation also begin to stir, and a few whispers are heard. Father Mark sits in the elegant pedestal of a chair along the left side of the altar. He rises slowly and walks across the white marble floor through the length of the altar. He steps up into the pulpit with a soft smile, adjusts the microphone to reach just under his chin, and silently prays for guidance for the startling message he is about to deliver.

He transitions into a bright Easter Sunday smile, and begins...

"Good morning, everyone," Father Mark opens his arms wide with a welcoming embrace. "How wonderful it is to have you all here. How wonderful it is to have a church at its capacity on this most blessed day. So, why is today so special? Why have so many of you come together to celebrate? Of course, Easter Sunday is a very special day, the day we celebrate the resurrection of our Lord Jesus Christ. This resurrection showed us that we will live again after our lives here on Earth. Our spirits will live again in the beauty of heaven. While I'm in no rush, I look forward to passing on and experiencing that.

"So, I have a question for everyone. Why is it that churches are not populated like this every week?" He opens his arms again, as if to embrace

3

the large crowd. "Why? I believe I know why." Father Mark pauses. "I suspect some of you are thinking 'Oh boy, he's going to scold us for not coming to church more often.' But, nope, I'm not going to do that. Do you know who I'm going to scold?"

Just before he answers his own question, he turns to the altar and again opens his arms and confesses, "Us! Because we, the leaders of the Catholic Church, have done a poor job of inspiring you."

He then turns back to face the congregation. "Really, that is the truth. Let's be honest. If you came here on Sundays and left inspired, wouldn't you come back more frequently? If, when you came here, we really helped you find your spirituality, wouldn't you feel more engaged with the Catholic Church? If we were less fear-and guilt-focused with our teachings, would you be more fulfilled in your participation? If we helped you discover who you are and what you truly believe, or if we helped you find your place in humanity, wouldn't you be happier and healthier people while here on this wonderful Earth?

"How many of your children leave here and tell you how bored they are? If you and your children received a message that was motivating, made you happier, challenged you, made you mentally stronger, made you more successful, made you more Christian-like, would you keep coming back?" Father Mark now raises his voice to say, "OF COURSE YOU WOULD," then quietly adds, "and so would your children. If teenagers came and received a message that uplifted them, would they complain so much about coming and spending about an hour each week with us? No, they wouldn't. Let me ask you: why did Jesus have so many followers? Because he inspired them. He taught them a new way to live. He didn't bore them with the same prayers every day, over and over. No, he delivered a message."

Both Father Frank and Monsignor Joseph frown and shift from side to side, visibly uncomfortable with Father Mark's message.

"So today, I'm going to tell you what I believe. Truth be told, well, I can't lie here!" There is some laughter from the congregation. "I had a restless night's sleep last night being apprehensive about delivering this message. But something made me feel an urgency to be candid. Divine guidance, I suppose. So, on this wonderful Easter Sunday, consider if you want to rise up like Jesus. Do you want to be that bright, beautiful light? Do you want to be happier? Do you want to be physically and mentally healthy? Do you want to shine outside because you shine inside? Do you want to achieve your goals? Do you want a more fulfilled relationship with your spouse, boyfriend or girlfriend, less sickness, or a happier family life? If you are contemplating 'yes' to any of these questions, I suggest you become more Christian-like."

The congregants are silent and seemingly transfixed awaiting his next words. He took a breath and continued. "Being Christian has nothing to do with being Catholic. I know we Catholic leaders are pretty good at communicating that the Catholic religion is the most relevant. We are also amazingly effective at instilling guilt."

Sitting in the fourth pew from the front in the left section is Jonathon Crew. Jonathon is a very successful writer for the New Jersey *Star-Ledger* and a well-respected journalist who's covered some of the tri-state's major events over the last twenty years: 9/11, Super Storm Sandy, Derek Jeter's 3,000th hit, New York Giants Super Bowls, to name a few. About 90 seconds into Father Mark's homily, he retrieves his iPhone and discreetly turns on the *record* button.

Father Mark continues. "Being a great Christian is not about following rules. It's about adhering to sound principles, such as helping one another, giving to the poor, donating your time, donating some of your money, teaching something valuable to someone, smiling, being generous, helping others, being truthful, being thankful in all things, and being a projector of a positive spirit. Be honest with others, even if you have to deliver a message that is hard for them to hear." Then he says quietly, as he realizes the impact this homily will have on these people, "As I am venturing to do right now.

"When I talk about being more Christian-like and questioning some of the rules of the Catholic Church, here's one I have struggled with for some time. Why is it if we REALLY BELIEVE that the Holy Spirit enters the host that we serve you—that this host REALLY is the body of Christ—then why must you be Catholic to receive it? Wouldn't we want everyone, regardless of their religious beliefs, to experience it? Why must you be part of the Catholic 'club' to receive Jesus?"

Some of the congregation begins to fidget in their seats. Expressions of disapproval move across their faces. Father Frank and Monsignor Joseph are looking even more uncomfortable. But some of the Mass attendees are nodding and smiling in approval. One mother of three takes out her iPhone and tweets ... *holy shit ftr mark of st.jude church is lashing out at the catholic church on easter.* Then she sends another tweet ... *and I LOVE it.* Even the teenagers in the congregation are paying attention. The standing-room-only crowd is fixed on Father Mark's message.

"So, here's what I'm going to do. I'm going to bless this host, as we do during every Mass and, as the spirit of Jesus enters it, offer it up to anyone who wants to be uplifted by this magnificent experience. I don't care if you're Jewish, Protestant, Lutheran, Buddhist, whatever. If you want to be uplifted by the body of Christ, then come and be uplifted." Then he added, "And for a change, this week, rather than donate your money to the Church, give it to someone else who needs it. Give it to the homeless, those who are impacted by disasters, disabled children, the elderly, and children struggling with cancer. Of course, we would like you to continue to support the Church but, honestly, the Catholic Church already has a lot of money. Did you know that while we don't report our financials, the Catholic Church has between 10 billion and 15 billion dollars in assets? We do some great things with those assets, but we can do better. There is nothing wrong with telling us that you're going do something different with your donations."

You could hear a pin drop as everyone sat waiting for Father Mark's next words. "I'm suggesting that we, the leaders of the Catholic Church, help you be comfortable with your spiritual liberty. This means that you can follow God and your spirituality the way you feel is best for you. These days, religion is under attack, and it may appear that this morning I'm attacking our religion; but what I'm trying to do is create awareness of changes we need to make. The moral principles of the Catholic Church are great, but the way they are communicated needs to be improved. One of the biggest concerns of our Catholic leaders is that society is losing its moral code. The media, TV, and Hollywood continue to deliver messages that the more things you have, the more sexual encounters you have, the more glamour you have, the more social media followers you have, the more money you have, the happier you'll be. Our desires must be met by self-discipline. We in the Catholic Church can help, but I feel HOW we do it needs to be drastically re-invented.

"I believe that men and women can too easily cross the line driven by desires, and we need to live more by spiritual principles that really bring happiness and success to all our lives. If we can transform how we inspire you and truly help you have a more fulfilled life, you will do the same more often with your children. There is nothing more important a parent can do than love their children and teach them proven, sound, spiritual principles. If we do this every day, we are creating a new positive cycle in our society. As I mentioned, we must maintain control of our desires. This is a principal theme in Buddhist teachings … that we, as people, will not find happiness in things, and we should be focused on the idea of less." Father Mark paused to let them take this in.

"If our children see us as material-focused, they will be the same. If they see us demonstrate envy, ego, and anger, they will do the same. But, if we guide them to be restrained and to use the principles of Christianity to guide their lives, they will achieve more happiness and contentment." We, as a Church, must show you how to remove the clutter and noise in your minds, to spend time just being still and quiet. We must guide you in how to have confidence and believe in yourself, how to be strong mentally and emotionally, to allow renewed thinking to open more doors to new possibilities, to believe in great things and have confidence in the face of challenges. We can empty out the negative and become open to the possibility of the new.

"So, we, the Catholic Church, need to wake up and realize we are losing our people. Between 2015 and 2020, Christians experienced the largest losses due to people leaving Christianity. Globally, about 5 million people became Christians in this 5-year period, while 13 million departed Christianity. Most of those who departed joined the ranks of the religiously unaffiliated. This points to the obvious issue we face. We are not inspiring people, so they drift away. We need to change our ways and reinvent ourselves."

A middle-aged man with a deep voice sitting in the middle of the congregation says out loud in approval: "AMEN!" With that, a woman sitting in the back-left corner of the church continues the support: "YES, AMEN."

Others, unhappy with Father Mark's message, attempt to "shush" the approvers. Many in attendance shift about nervously, making eye contact with no one. Then a man says loud enough for most to hear, "This is unacceptable;" while a woman behind him retorts, "No it's not. Finally, someone is speaking up." An elderly woman with silver grey hair sitting in the third-to-last pew hastily stands up and shuffles quickly in front of five or six other congregants to walk out of the church. A few others follow.

Father Mark raises his hands above his shoulders with his palms facing the congregation. "It's okay. Everyone is entitled to his or her reaction," he says. Then he pauses in silence for about five seconds with his hands remaining above his head.

Jonathan Crew, the *Star Ledger* writer, checks his iPhone to be sure it's still recording everything. He looks around him and, to his surprise, he notices several other people also recording the event.

Father Mark continues as he lowers his arms and rests his hands on the pulpit railings. "All I'm trying to say is that the Church is not getting it completely right. You all are not getting it quite right," he continues, as he points to the large congregation. "We (and he turns to the priests now sitting very uncomfortably on each side of the altar) are not getting it right. Want to get it right? Don't come here next Sunday. Really! Don't come. Instead, go feed the poor, go to a big city and find a homeless person and buy them food to eat. Go to one of the elderly homes nearby and visit strangers and make them smile. Comfort another living being who is less fortunate. Not only will you feel better than you do leaving church on Sunday, you will be an embodiment of Jesus. You will be doing his work.

"So, why today? Why on this Easter Sunday do I express what may seem a controversial point of view? I'm not certain, but maybe the spirit has moved me on this most blessed day. Maybe because, as usual on Easter, we have a full church, and I want to communicate my message to as many as I can. Or maybe I have just gotten to the point where I needed to express these thoughts and feelings."

Father Mark is about to finish his homily but has one more very important thing to get off his chest.

"As I conclude, I need to express one more very important point." He pauses again for a few seconds, then speaks. "I'm sorry. I'm very sorry for what the Catholic Church has done to hurt so many children. I truly am sorry. The abuse is horrible. The cover-up is a disgrace. I bring this up because I know the behavior of many within the Catholic Church has kept some of you from regularly attending church. I completely understand this. Many have told me that they have a very difficult time coming to church knowing priests have preyed on young boys and caused them lasting harm. When I posed the question at the beginning of this homily, asking why is it that so many of you are here today but don't come often, I know this horrible situation is one of the reasons.

"Through this very difficult time for the Catholic Church, I'm grateful to the many great Catholic leaders who have done wonderful things for so many people around the world. I just want us to get it right more often. And it starts here, by inspiring you and by making you feel your power, the power that God gave you. God's power is in each and every one of you, and you can use it to create good in the world."

"I tell the children here," now Father Mark raises his voice and spreads his arms out wide with palms facing everyone, mirroring the same position as Jesus's on the cross, "you can be anything you want to be as long as you work hard for it, pay the price, believe in yourself, ask God for help, and think positively. I repeat, ask God for help. See yourself as though you already are what you want to be, and you will become that. I (and he says loudly) PROMISE you. Remember, Jesus told us *You can do even greater things than these.*" Then he again pauses a few seconds and softly says, "Thank you for listening, and I wish you a very happy and blessed Easter."

As Father Mark turns around, steps down the two steps from the altar podium and walks toward his place at the altar, a woman stands up and shouts, "Yes, sir" and claps, and almost immediately so do about seventy percent of the congregation, and some even whistle. Others who are not supportive sit stone-faced. As Father Mark listens to the volume of ovation behind him, he looks over at his fellow priests on the altar and observes looks of censure on their faces. He knows he has gone to a place that he may not be able to reverse.

CHAPTER 2

The congregation is now at home. While preparing their Easter festivities, some are simultaneously on the phone with friends and relatives explaining the odd but inspirational sermon they just experienced. Others are touting it via email or tweets, and a few are even putting recorded segments on YouTube and their Facebook page for the world to experience.

Jonathan Crew is at his PC franticly writing his Monday story as his wife calls him to help carve the veal loin she prepared. The headline reads: HAPPY EASTER—PRIEST AGGRESSIVELY CHALLENGES THE CATHOLIC CHURCH DURING EASTER SERMON.

Monday morning arrives with the *Star Ledger*'s front-page headline and story of Father Mark's Easter message. The story blends a supportive acceptance to the message with the question of "What motivated this sermon?" The story impacted the thinking of many.

Several local and national news outlets around the country picked up and covered the story. Tweets abounded on the internet by supporters and detractors alike. The war of words represented the very issue Father Mark alluded to in what will be his historic Easter sermon.

Within a few days, Father Mark has gotten over 1,000 emails almost evenly split between supporters and angry detractors. Some emails are ugly, predicting Father Mark will go to Hell for disrespecting the Catholic Church. Others applaud him for his bravery and for communicating a message many felt should have been delivered long ago. As he sits and reads the emails, tweets, and even texts to his cell phone, he wonders what he has created. He can't believe his verbal "blog" is receiving this much attention. He buries his face in his hands, as he prays for guidance.

It's Wednesday afternoon and Father Mark is summoned by Monsignor Joseph to his office in the rectory behind the church. Monsignor Joseph is in his late sixties but very fit. He runs three times each week on the shore side boardwalk and even hits the gym occasionally. He sports a full head of gray hair and is downright handsome. Copies of the New Jersey *Star Ledger*, *Connecticut Print*, *NY Daily News*, *Illinois Gazette*, and, yes, even the *New York Times* that have covered the Easter chat sit in front of him on his desk. Monsignor Joseph gestures for Father Mark to sit down and, as Father Mark obliges, the Monsignor asks, "Did you enjoy your Easter?"

"Yes, I did. I took a long walk on the beach and then had dinner at a friend's house in Franklin Lakes. A very relaxing day, other than the holiday traffic. How about you?"

"Yes, a very enjoyable holiday. As you know, I went to visit my sister and her family upstate. I just got back this morning. It felt good to get away for a few days."

Monsignor points to the newspapers on his desk. "Now, let's talk about this serious situation. Why did you do this? What's going on?"

Father Mark is confident. "I just wanted to be honest. This came from my heart."

Monsignor is inquisitive. "So, you don't want people to come to church? We're boring? We don't inspire anyone?"

Father Mark interrupts, "Come on, Monsignor, do you really think you inspire people every Sunday? They come on Sunday mostly because of obligation. Yes, some few understand the beauty of the Mass, but they lose it through the mundane delivery we give."

He leans forward, "The truth is, we stink." Now, he stands up and paces the room. "I want to touch the hearts and souls of these people. We are here to do what Jesus did—to motivate, inspire, help make this world a better place, and teach the people to help solve the world's problems so we can have what God intended for us.

"People come and go every Sunday with little improvement. The truth is, we are losing people. They don't want to be here. The children don't want to be here." Father Mark waves his arms in disgust. "You know, Monsignor," he says pointing out the window to his right, "those in the Vatican don't even get it right."

Monsignor Joseph then stands up from behind his desk and firmly requests that Mark sit down. Father Mark obliges and the Monsignor returns to his chair. "We both know you come from a very different background and experience than 99 percent of Catholic priests, and that difference usually allows you to have a valuable perspective." The Monsignor is firm in his voice. "That said, there is a better way for you to communicate that perspective. I would like you to retract your statements. You can retract them and say you didn't mean them literally."

Father Mark interrupts, "But I did mean them that way."

The Monsignor continues as though he didn't hear a word from Father Mark. "You say that you know the Church does wonderful things in this world, that the Mass is sacred, and participating in the Mass strengthens spirituality."

Father Mark interrupts again and says, "I already said that during my homily."

Monsignor Joseph leans forward. "You tell them that you got caught up in the spirit of Easter and went too far."

Then there is a pause in the room and both stay silent. Monsignor Joseph is wondering if he is affecting Father Mark. His expression is hopeful.

Father Mark leans back in his chair. "I'm sorry, Monsignor, I can't do that. I would be lying."

Monsignor Joseph again stands up and paces the length of his mahogany desk, then turns toward Father Mark. "Then you need to take some time off and think about this further. You are acting like a rebel, and we can't have this. We love your desire and enthusiasm, but you cannot go off and make the statements you have made. Take a few days and come back and tell me what you're thinking. You know my expectations." As he finishes this sentence, the Monsignor walks in front of Mark and extends his hand, wanting to shake hands in agreement.

Father Mark stands up and, instead of shaking his hand, he hugs Monsignor Joseph and says, "I understand."

Father Mark leaves the rectory and decides to head to the beach. Today is a pleasant 62 degrees with the sun shining. Children are in school and parents are busy at work, so the beach is empty.

A Single Day of Peace

Father Mark removes his black shoes and socks, stuffs one sock into each shoe, picks up his shoes and walks down six steps from the boardwalk to the beach. His bare feet absorb the cool beach sand. He walks the full width of the beach to the surf's edge. The beach always has a sanative effect on him. The cool sand feels good on his feet. He rolls up each pant leg to just below his knees. He carries his shoes dangling in his right hand as he walks north with each wave's last ripple greeting his feet. There is a chill in the sea this time of the year, but it feels refreshing. The ocean looks particularly blue today; very clear.

The surf has just the right number of waves that a surfer enjoys. As he strolls, he looks out over the ocean and sees four or five surfers lying on their boards waiting for the next wave. Here comes one, and they paddle feverishly to catch the exact right moment of this wave's life, and three are successful at catching it for a stimulating ride. They surf the wave in a line next to each other as if they practiced this choreography a thousand times. Father Mark speaks out loud to himself as he watches. "Wonderful to see the beauty of people doing what they love." As he continues to walk, he replays in his mind the Easter sermon and the meeting he just had with Monsignor Joseph. He prays for guidance.

CHAPTER 3

Mark Tossi was born and raised in New Jersey. He grew up in a very supportive, middle-class family. His mother, a driven person, always encouraged Mark to be and do anything he set his heart on... as long as he committed to working hard. His father, however, was a bit more conservative and, while supportive, avoided risk at all times.

Since his younger years, Mark always had a curiosity about God and even considered becoming a priest. While Mark enjoyed being inspired to learn about and potentially spread God's word, he also found that he had the mind of a businessperson. He liked the idea of building an enterprise and making money! Growing up in a middle-class family in the 1970s, he yearned for more. His father and mother always provided well for the family, but money concerns occurred often. Mark wanted to live differently. He wanted the good things in life and to not experience the pressures of the constant shortage of money... within reason. He didn't feel he needed to be the wealthiest person in the land, but financial independence was his goal.

As Mark entered his senior year in college, he knew he had a decision to make. Should he pursue a career in business or dedicate himself to promote spirituality? After thinking long and hard and praying on the topic, the voice inside guided him to follow his business aspirations.

Upon graduating with a degree in business, he interviewed with many companies in search of his first professional employment. He found that the technology industry intrigued him. He had several successful interviews at IBM and hoped he would be selected to join their sales training academy. This program selected recent college graduates and trained them to be successful sales professionals—the IBM way. Mark did receive the offer and started his career at IBM.

While at IBM, he met Stephanie Winslet who would be the love of his life. Stephanie, an Irish Catholic with some Italian in her heritage, proved to be a masterful marketer and led a marketing team within IBM. She often supported the sales team at conferences and trade shows. Mark got to know Stephanie and, before long, they became a serious couple.

Two years later, Mark and Stephanie married and within four years they had two boys, first Richard and then Dylan. At first Stephanie struggled with the decision to leave IBM and become a stay-at-home mother. She found herself not completely fulfilled leaving behind her marketing prowess. This all changed when she decided to do freelance consulting and helped other companies with their marketing challenges. Before long, her practice took off and she felt she achieved the perfect balance of motherhood and professional.

With Mark's career on the rise, he often found it difficult to balance the desires and responsibilities of being a father, along with the commitment required to be a successful sales executive. Also difficult on the family had been the three re-locations Mark accepted as part of the promotions he received—from New York to Atlanta and then to Chicago. During ten years at IBM, Mark had grown to Senior VP of Global Sales for the fastest growing division at IBM, the Data Analytics Division.

While his career and earnings skyrocketed, he remained true to his faith and prayed daily, attended church almost every Sunday, and enjoyed being a lector at Mass. His spirituality and connection with God kept him grounded, as he played in the big game of technology business. Then in the middle of the summer of 2017, Mark received a call from an executive recruiter representing an early-stage artificial intelligence software company named Blend-AI. Blend-AI needed to replace the technology-focused founder with an experienced and sales-driven CEO. Along with two other executives, Mark had been identified as a top candidate by the lead venture capital firm that funded Blend-AI. While very happy in Chicago leading IBM's most successful software division, Mark always wanted to join a start-up to see if he could be one of those Silicon Valley winners. Blend-AI, however, did not reside in Silicon Valley; the headquarters had a New York City address.

That evening at the dinner table of their beautiful five-bedroom 5,700 square foot duplex home in the Lincoln Park section of Chicago, Mark explained to Stephanie that this opportunity had been presented to him. He explained that the interview process would be challenging and, while he might not be offered the position, he wanted to investigate it. As a big company guy, most early-stage companies didn't look positively on executives from that segment. The start-up and early-stage world often wondered if the big company executive could adapt to the fast pace, ever-changing, and often budget-constrained, growth-driven company. It intrigued Mark that if successful in being selected for this CEO position, they could move back to their home state of New Jersey.

Stephanie felt a bit skeptical because Mark had done so well at IBM and still had a very bright future there. After much productive debate, they both agreed they would take it one step at a time and start with one interview back in New York City. If this did become serious and Mark decided to take this new role with relocation, Stephanie could continue her consulting practice back east. Several of her clients had offices in the tri-state area, so this could have a positive impact on her as well.

On a blustery cold Chicago morning in February, Mark boarded a United flight out of O'Hare Airport to Newark New Jersey's Liberty National Airport to attend his interview with Blend-AI. During the flight, he felt oddly calm about it all. He prayed about it and had a comfortable feeling that this was the right thing to do. The voice inside told him he would be moving back to New Jersey soon.

The day with Blend-AI proved to be hectic as it had back-to-back interviews, including lunch and dinner meetings. Mark met with each of the senior leadership team members, some of the salespeople, and three partners from PureVentures, the lead venture capital firm that invested over $45M in the company. PureVentures certainly had a big stake in Blend-AI being successful.

Mark felt impressed with every aspect of Blend-AI except for how they marketed their core value proposition. He knew if they were going to be successful and grow from their current $20M revenue position to $100M or more, they had to significantly change how they positioned themselves to the world regarding the problems they solved. This was critical to them becoming the category leader by uniquely defining how they approached the business problem they solved.

Blend-AI used big data, machine learning, and artificial intelligence (AI) to help companies in all industries serve their customers more successfully. Combining their unique AI capabilities with the expertise of experienced customer service representatives gave Blend-AI clients a powerful competitive advantage. Blend-AI's clients served their customers better than anyone in their market segment, because they could anticipate in advance what problems or questions the clients would have before they knew they had them.

On the late-night flight home from Newark to Chicago, Mark Tossi knew he wanted the CEO job at Blend-AI.

CHAPTER 4

Stephanie had fallen sound asleep by the time Mark returned to their duplex. She had had a very long day of conference calls with her clients and had fallen into a very restful sleep. Mark entered their home through the front door after being dropped off by an Uber. He tried to be very quiet as he moved around the first floor but, when he walked into one of the kitchen chairs left jutting away from the granite island countertop, Stephanie jumped up from her slumber. Realizing Mark was downstairs, she got out of bed and went down to receive the news on how the day went at Blend-AI.

Mark took her through all the details and Stephanie could see in Mark's tone, body language and the serious look in his eyes that he wanted that job. He desired that challenge. She went over to Mark, gave him a hug and whispered, "I'll start getting mentally ready to move to New Jersey." Then she gave him a kiss and said, "Time for bed, we both had a long day, and I'm sure you have a full schedule tomorrow."

The next morning, Mark woke at his customary time of 5:15 a.m. but, today, before going straight to the gym in his home, he went to his office on the first floor and settled in front of his PC which sat on a beautiful oak desk. He opened his personal Gmail account and intended to send thank you emails to everyone he met yesterday at Blend-AI.

Much to his surprise, there are two interesting emails in his inbox. One from the founder and current CEO of Blend-AI, and the other from the VC partner who is a member of Blend-AI's Board of Directors. Both stated how thankful they are that Mark visited them in New York City, and they wanted to arrange a conference call sometime that afternoon to discuss the next steps.

Mark knew what that meant. He did well yesterday, and they are seriously interested in him. He replied quickly, offered several time slots in the afternoon for a thirty-minute call, and pressed "send" with the emotion of an NFL star who just scored a touchdown on a Sunday afternoon. He followed that email up with the appropriate "thank you" emails to all the people he met at Blend-AI. He then proceeded to his gym and had an energetic work out.

Blend-AI's CEO and board member selected 2:30 p.m. Central time for the call. Mark began to feel uneasy. He had learned to listen to that voice inside him, and he wondered what the inner voice is telling him. In deep thought, he sat back in the large black leather chair in his corner office and gazed out his window overlooking the large office complex. He stood up, walked to the office door, and asked Alisa, his assistant, to not interrupt him for a few minutes. As Mark closed the door, Alisa had a sense as to what would be going on. After all, she had been his assistant for over three years, and they enjoyed a fun and productive working relationship. She knew this is Mark's way of saying, *I'm going to meditate quietly for a few minutes.* Mark often meditated when he had big decisions to make, was facing a challenge, or had a great success take place.

Mark walked back to his comfortable black leather chair, sat in a relaxed way, closed his eyes and took three deep breaths. In his mind, he went through the meditation process he had become certified in years ago by the Silva Method. The Silva Method was created by Jose Silva and, as Mark told many people, made all the difference in his life. The power of visualization, meditation, and positive affirmations allowed Mark to stay humble while he created his own destiny.

This time, rather than repeating his goals and seeing himself achieving them, he just stayed silent and asked one question in his mind, "Why am I feeling uneasy?" After relaxing silently for approximately ten minutes, Mark opened his eyes and, as if he received an injection of a B12 shot, he sprang up wide-awake and energetic. He walked back to his office door, opened it and then returned to his desk.

That indicated to Alisa that Mark completed his quiet time. It had been just the amount of time as usual. Alisa got up, walked to Mark's doorway and said, "Anything I can help you with?"

Mark said, "No thank you, Alisa. All good."

"I see on your calendar you have a private call coming up at 2:30. Can I get you anything for that call?" Alisa asked.

Mark's odd look and his response, "No, I'm good," sent a message to Alisa. She knew Mark inside and out and had a feeling something would be different about this call. She then turned around and walked back to her desk.

Mark felt very satisfied and confident, like someone had whispered the secret of life into his mind during his meditation. Then he spoke softly out loud to himself, "That is it. I had been too aggressive in my desire for this call and new opportunity. Just chill and be professional and let it play out to God's will." He was pleased with the divine message his inner voice gave him during his silence. He felt ready for his 2:30 call.

At exactly 2:25, Alisa went to Mark's office door and quietly closed it to give him privacy for the call. She didn't say a word and walked to her desk wondering what might be up. "Ah, it's nothing," she thought. "Probably something for the church, his son's high school baseball team, or something like that." Mark had a successful history of fundraising for the church and his son's sports teams.

At 2:29 p.m., Mark dialed into the arranged conference line for the call with Blend-AI's founder Evan Lyons and Sean Dawkins, the board member from PureVentures. Promptly at 2:30 p.m., Sean Dawkins joined the conference call and began. "Mark, thanks so much for making time this afternoon to speak with us. Everyone really enjoyed the meetings with you yesterday, and we wanted to recap everything. Evan should be on the line any minute." Mark shared with Sean that he, too, felt the meetings went exceptionally well, and he left with a very positive feeling about the potential to work together.

After further pleasantries and small talk, the time reached 2:37 and Evan hadn't joined the call yet. Sean wanted to get things going. "I'm sorry, Mark, but Evan seems to be delayed a bit with some business. You know these founders; they beat to their own drum!"

Mark chuckled and said, "It's not like I've never been late to a conference call. It's no problem." Just then, a beep in the line sounded, and Evan stated, "Sorry I'm late guys. How's everyone today?"

The call went on for an efficient twelve minutes. As Mark hung up the phone, he sat back in his chair and looked at his office wall displaying the many awards he received at IBM. Then he said aloud, "Wow! Looks like I may be leaving here."

He then picked up his cell phone and called Stephanie. "Hey Steph, got a minute? I just got off the phone with the guys at Blend-AI, and they want to move fast with checking my references, and if that goes well, they want me back in NYC to discuss terms of employment as their CEO." Stephanie smiled, and Mark could hear and feel the smile. While she didn't say anything, Mark said, "Thank you. I love you."

Then Stephanie said, "I'll see you after 7 p.m. for dinner. I'll have the boys wait to eat with us. You have some information to share with them." Then, just before they both hung up, Stephanie interrupted and said, "Mark, wait. You probably should have a chat with Alisa. She will read you a mile away, and it's better you give her a heads-up sooner than later. You know you can trust her."

"Yeah, you're right. Will do. See you later. Love you."

Mark walked to his office door, opened it, and asked Alisa to come in. She now knew it wasn't a church or high school sports call Mark had taken. She walked in, sat on the couch in his office, and he sat across from her on a fashionable office chair. He began to explain. While Alisa, the consummate professional, tried to remain balanced in her expression, she couldn't hold back her surprised look as Mark outlined what had transpired the last few weeks. To her, Mark represented "Mr. IBM" and the idea of him considering leaving the company had her feeling a sense of shock.

At dinner that evening, the family engaged in the usual conversation of school, sports, and the New York Yankees upcoming spring training—the Tossi family are die-hard Yankee fans. When it wasn't baseball season and they couldn't root for the men in pinstripes, they tracked winter meetings, free agent signings, and trades. Mark then transitioned the dinner conversation as he did in many executive meetings. He moved it away from the casual fun conversation to a tone of seriousness. Mark began with a question for Richard and Dylan. "Hey guys, if you had something new happen to you that you were really jazzed about, would you want me and mom to know about it?"

21

Richard, who had Mark's quick thinking and wit, said, "Only if it didn't have anything to do with some new girl I'm interested in!"

They laughed, but Dylan looked a bit embarrassed. Dylan is more like his mother ... sensitive, loving, and always seeing the other person's perspective.

Mark continued, "Okay, but seriously, if you had something that could be special in your life, wouldn't you want to share it even before everything had been finalized, like your excited and you want me and Mom to be part of the excitement and possibility?"

Dylan spoke up and said, "Sure Dad, like that time I heard the head travel baseball coach for the Knights had interest in me playing for them and, although I haven't gotten a call yet, I talked to you and Mom about it."

"Exactly," Mark said with approval. Then again, as a senior executive does very well, Mark got to the point. "Okay, let's cut to the chase and let me tell you what may be exciting in my life and yours."

Mark went on to explain all the details of what had gone on during the last few weeks. This was followed by a thirty-minute question and answer session addressing all of Richard's and Dylan's questions, talking through the challenges of high school students moving to a new city and school, new sports teams, and making new friends. The conversation ended with concern from the boys but anticipation, too.

Mark's final words, "Okay, now it is really, really, REALLY important that you don't go talking about this to anyone just yet. I don't know if I will get the position, and I have to be respectful to IBM and let them know before they hear any rumors. Rumors spread fast, so if you tell a friend about this, it can easily find its way to someone at IBM, and I don't want my company getting word before I tell them. I don't want that to happen ... okay?" The boys agreed and Mark felt comfortable that he could trust them.

After dinner, the boys went to their rooms to do their homework, and Stephanie approached Mark while he responded to emails on his iPad. She started to say, "You know Mark..."

But Mark interrupted, as he knew exactly what Stephanie wanted to say. "Yes, I know. I need to tell Bruce ASAP." Bruce McMichaels was Mark's boss and senior vice-president at IBM. "I will sit him down tomorrow and explain everything and let him know that, while things aren't finalized, he deserves to know what has been going on."

CHAPTER 5

The next morning while Mark enjoyed a brisk workout in his home gym, he sent a text to Bruce McMichaels. *Hey, Bruce, can we get thirty minutes today to chat about something?* Within twenty seconds Mark's phone pinged with the tone indicating the receipt of a text message. *Sure, I'll have Susan arrange a time and let you know.*

The day proceeded as typical for Mark with several sales meetings, contract negotiations, and a 45-minute welcome speech to a group of 36 new hires. Mark's division experienced significant growth and every other month he had a new group of salespeople, sales operations specialists, and sales development representatives joining the business.

After today's talk to the new-hire group, Mark felt particularly uneasy, because he felt he misled them a bit. He talked all about the history of this division, how it had significant double-digit growth over the last five years, how the future would continue to be bright and how, as a team, they always had to be sure they leveraged each other's strengths to ensure success, no matter how large they became. And to never forget that they existed to serve their clients.

Mark felt exhausted after this talk, because he knew that if he got the new CEO position, he would be resigning, and those 36 people would think he misled them, speaking so highly of the company and the opportunity in front of them. He whispered to himself, "I have to figure this out ASAP, because I can't keep juggling like this."

Just then, Mark's phone buzzed with a text from Bruce's assistant Susan. *Mark, can you come by Bruce's office at 5:15 today?* Mark's emoji of a "thumbs up" indicated he would be there.

"What's happening my man?" Bruce McMichaels asked, as Mark walked into Bruce's office promptly at 5:15 p.m. Mark closed the door behind him, and Bruce said, "Oh boy, this must be serious. Did you just close a multi-million-dollar deal?"

Mark replied as he sat down at the chair across from Bruce's desk, "Well, maybe, but not that kind of deal for IBM." Bruce looked up with a confused expression. Mark began, "Bruce, I need to talk to you about something that is going on. Nothing is final, but I feel you should know what I'm doing. You know how I always talked about doing a start-up at some point, and how I wanted to see if I could take my big company experience and use it to help a new company succeed?"

"You're *leaving* us?" Bruce interrupted while emphasizing the word LEAVING.

"No, no, not yet. A VC for a company called Blend-AI contacted me, we chatted a few times, and I liked what I heard. Last week, I went to visit them in New York City, and it went great. They called me back and want to pursue references. It's all happening so quickly. It feels right, but I don't have an offer, so I don't know how this will end."

Bruce rose from his chair and walked behind where Mark was sitting. Mark paused to see if Bruce's stroll would have him arrive back within his line of sight. After about ten seconds of silence and no view of Bruce, Mark turned around and said, "Where did you go?"

"Ah, shit! Mark," Bruce said as he resumed his walk to the other side of his desk and stood there looking at Mark. "This really sucks. I mean, I want you to do what's right for you, Stephanie, and the kids, but, shit, you have a great thing going on here."

Mark responded, "Yes, I know that. I know. But I'm just going to see this through and pray on it. I will keep you posted every step along the way. Do you want to tell John?" John Willis is the division president.

"No, not now. You know how he reacts to things. Let's just let it sit for now and, depending on what happens next, we can decide what to tell him, if anything at all."

"Will do. I understand."

With that, Susan walked in and said, "Bruce, you have to get going to get to your dinner with Blue Star."

"Yep. I'm leaving now." With that, Bruce gave Mark his fist for a fist pump and said, "Go kick some ass. Let's talk tomorrow."

The next seven days felt like a whirlwind for Mark. As expected, his references provided glowing recommendations to Blend-AI; even Bruce spoke to them on Mark's behalf.

While all progressed well with Blend-AI, Mark recognized that his sons became very argumentative over the last few days, particularly Dylan. They were feeling the effects of a possible move to an unknown area. The thought of leaving their friends and sports teams is causing them stress. Stephanie continued to tell Mark that she would take care of the boys through this uncertain time, and he needed to focus on making the right decision for everyone. Mark felt the stress, too. To him, the family's happiness is most important. He knew that some of the best decisions started with stress but, in time, they proved to be the right direction. He always felt that every ending had a new beginning.

Mark flew back to New York so they could discuss the economics of the offer and then, within twenty-four hours, a written offer arrived in Mark's personal Gmail. The night he received the offer, he became more anxious. He knew this is now for real. Decision time. He walked from his home office into the kitchen where Stephanie is making green tea. "Well, it's show time. I got the offer. They gave me just about everything I asked for."

Calmly, Stephanie continued to pour the hot water from the teapot into her favorite mug that had the word "Family" painted on it, put the teapot down on the stove, walked up very close to Mark, gently put her hands on either side of his face, and said, "I love you. We are good no matter what you decide."

Mark then said, "What WE decide."

"Listen, my love," Stephanie often called him that, "while it is a family decision, it is your decision because it impacts your career, your day-to-day. Me and the boys support you one hundred percent." With that, she kissed him gently on his lips and walked over to get her tea.

Mark responded, "I'll pray again for guidance and the strength to make the right decision and will sleep on it. Tomorrow morning, I'll know."

CHAPTER 6

Three weeks to the day since he received the formal CEO offer from Blend-AI, Mark entered the Chicago Cut Steakhouse on North LaSalle for his going-away dinner. He expertly navigated the process of finalizing his acceptance with Blend-AI as well as the resignation process and transition out of IBM. Now, it is time to say goodbye to those he worked with so closely. Over 100 of his employees and co-workers came to the event—by invitation only—and the private room with richly wooden paneled walls buzzed with positive energy. While everyone felt sad because of Mark's departure, they all felt very happy for what the future could bring him. Some hoped that he would take them along to his new company.

Donna Barbaris, one of the top sales performers in Mark's division, came up to him with her glass of Reposado tequila on the rocks in hand. "Mark, I want to tell you something. You did something very special yesterday. You brought in the 36 new recruits to a meeting and explained that when you gave them your original welcome speech, you were considering this new opportunity. You wanted them to know that while the situation was unique, you believed in what you told them. You explained the uncomfortable feeling you experienced during the talk since you had been pursuing another opportunity. That move, that gesture is what you're all about. I know it meant a lot to those people. They felt relieved with your honesty. They really appreciated it."

"Thanks, Donna. I'm going to miss you."

"No, you're not," Donna replied, "because you're going to bring me with you!" With a smile and a wink, she walked away.

Just then, Bruce McMichaels took a spoon in his right hand and, as he held his glass of red wine by the stem in his left hand, he raised the glass up above his shoulder and began to tap it with the spoon to get everyone's attention. Then, as if on cue, everyone joined in tapping their glasses. It sounded like a well-orchestrated series of bells ringing. After about fifteen seconds of glasses ringing, Bruce raised his right hand very high as if to say,

"Enough. Quiet please." Being six foot five, his hand could easily be seen by all.

When silence came over the room, Bruce began. "Well, it's time for the man of the hour to share a few words with us. But, before he does, I want to say something and propose a toast. Mark, thank you for everything you have done here at IBM. You have been a role model for so many. Your positive spirit, your encouragement, your mentoring, your 'can do' attitude, your toughness, and, yes, even your cursing from time to time"—many chuckled at this, because Mark had a tendency to drop a few expletives— "all that you are about has made us all better business people and better human beings. Me included. So, everyone, please raise your glass, and I want to wish Mark the best of luck at Blend-AI and wish him and his family much success and happiness as they move back home to New Jersey."

With that, many shouts of "To Mark" could be heard as everyone raised their glass and took a drink, followed by loud calls for, "SPEECH, SPEECH!"

The room became very quiet as Mark cleared his throat, held his wine glass in his left hand, and began to speak. "Every ending has a new beginning. Some of you have heard me say that from time to time. We tend to be sad at endings, because we're leaving behind something that has become part of us. It could be a vacation where you had a wonderful time and now you're leaving that beautiful hotel and headed to the airport to get back home, life, and work. Maybe it's the ending of a course you took that changed how you will cook, or an ending of a great book you are read or saying goodbye to a close friend who is moving away. Or, of course, the ending of a job as you move forward to the next one.

"This ending is a new beginning for me and all of you. My beginning will be to take on a totally new challenge as I advance my career and try to make a significant, positive difference to Blend-AI. It is a new beginning for you as well. You will have new leadership, new ways to do things, new and probably better ideas to propel you and the company further. Newness and change don't always feel good in the beginning. It can be unsettling and stressful."

Many nodded in agreement, several with tears in their eyes. "But, if we take that new thing and see it, visualize it for the good it will bring, it lessens the anxiety a bit. For me, I know this newness will put me in new circumstances, even though today I have no idea what they will be. But I trust in God that it will all be better for me and those around me. My leaving is a great opportunity for all of you. It's an opportunity for you to change and experience new things—new positive things.

"Without mentioning any names, because there are way too many to mention and I know I will forget some, I will just extend a big warm, loving and heartfelt"— Mark put his right hand over his left chest to as to touch his heart— "THANK YOU to everyone who has worked with and for me here at IBM. I have so much gratitude for you all.

"Together we innovated, laughed, cried, won, lost, succeeded, failed, ran, walked, stressed, and relaxed. A life is fulfilling not because of the things you acquire. It is fulfilling because of the people you touch and who touch you. You have touched me so deeply, and I hope I've done the same for you. Again, THANK YOU. And here's to every ending having a new beginning!" With that, Mark raised his left hand, holding up a glass of cabernet to make a toast. Everyone followed and raised their glasses and drank.

Mark enjoyed the evening with much reminiscing, sharing stories, laughs, and more tears. Many shared with Mark how he contributed to their success. One thanked him for all the books he recommended they read, another for teaching her about meditation, another for recommending yoga and, of course, many for the great business and leadership lessons he taught them.

No one wanted to leave, but by 10:30 p.m. many began to filter out to get home. By this time, Mark felt emotionally drained. He found himself frequently praying to himself during the evening to acquire the strength to stay emotionally stable. While he knew he is experiencing a new beginning, deep down he felt sadness. These people had been his extended family. He felt love for them.

When Mark arrived home, Stephanie greeted him and said, "You look very tired, Mark. How did it go?"

Mark took off his coat and walked over to the hallway closet. "It went great. That is an amazing group of people. The laughs, the tears, the stories. It felt great but I'm drained. I need a good night's sleep."

CHAPTER 7

Two weeks after Mark's resignation party, he arrived in New York seriously engaged in his new role as the CEO of Blend-AI. Back in Chicago, Stephanie and the two boys continued their routine. Until the high school year completed in 45 days, they would stay in Chicago while Mark commuted to New York. He would be in New York City Monday through Friday and then back to Chicago on Friday night to Sunday evening. Then back to New York. When school ended for summer break, Stephanie and the boys will move to New Jersey while Stephanie's great friend, Megan, an expert residential real estate agent, would sell their home.

This first week at Blend-AI coincided with a two-day meeting with the board of directors. This gave Mark a chance to collaborate with both the board and his leadership team on the critical planning that needed to be done for the second half of the fiscal year.

Just after 2:30 p.m., Lisa Denmark, one of Blend-AI's board of directors and a proven marketing expert, was presenting new, compelling marketing ideas to Blend's board and executive staff.

During Lisa's presentation, Mark's assistant, Alexa, hurried into the conference room. Obviously upset, she rushed over to Evan Lyons, the founder and newly appointed chief technology officer of Blend-AI. She whispered something in his ear and pulled at his right shirtsleeve as if to say, "You have to come with me now."

Evan got up and said, "Excuse me everyone. I'll be right back." He left the conference room and Lisa continued to present her marketing ideas. Within three minutes, Evan returned and visually upset. He walked up to Sean Dawkins, a board member and partner at PureVentures, who actively recruited Mark to Blend-AI, and whispered into his ear, "Please come with me. It's an emergency." Then Evan spoke up and said, "Lisa, sorry to interrupt you. Peter, can you please come with me?" Peter Cardova is another board member seated at the large boardroom table. Sean didn't wait for Peter's response, as he walked out of the conference room. Peter left following Sean to Evan's office.

Mark then spoke up, "Something is obviously going on, so why don't we take a fifteen-minute break? What Lisa is presenting is far too important for many of the team to miss." They all agreed. Some decided to leave the room to stretch their legs, and others went to the back of the boardroom to refresh their coffee, snack on the platter of assorted cookies, or grab a bottle of water.

Mark walked out of the conference room and down the hall and reached an area where he could see through the glass wall of Evan's office. He saw his assistant Alexa crying, and both Sean Dawkins and Peter Cardova had an expression of shock and disbelief. They could see Mark walking toward them and, as Mark looked at their expressions, he became overwhelmed with a feeling of fear.

Without thinking, he walked right into the office. Alexa was sobbing as she sat in a chair. Evan had his right arm around her shoulders to console her. Sean Dawkins began to speak and did so with fear in his voice. "Mark, there has been a terrible accident in Chicago with your family. It appears to be very serious. You need to get back to Chicago right away."

Mark responded with rapid questions, "Are they okay? Are they hurt? What happened? Where are they?"

Sean replied. "I don't know what happened. Alexa got a call from the Chicago police, and they are trying to locate you. Then your friend Josh Moller called right after and said for you to call him as you're going to the airport. I don't want to speculate on anything. You need to talk to the police right away. Stay right here and let me go talk to Lisa for a minute." Sean rushed out and Mark realized he had left his cell phone in the conference room, so he ran out of Evan's office and ran past Sean, arriving to the conference room first.

He rushed over to get his iPhone which remained on silent mode and saw he missed many calls from Josh Moller and another Chicago based number. As Mark picked up his phone to call Josh back, Sean explained to everyone in the room there had been a very serious accident with Mark's family, and he needed to fly back ASAP. Everyone in the room immediately became silent with disbelief.

31

As Sean continued to explain, Mark walked quickly out of the conference room looking at his phone and clicking on recent calls. With his hands shaking, he clicked Josh's number to call him back. Then, putting the iPhone to his ear as Josh answered. "Josh, what's going on? Are they okay?" Mark paused to listen, as he quickly walked into his office. "What do you mean all you know is there has been a bad accident, and everyone has been rushed to the hospital? Don't you know what happened? Where are you now? Please get to the hospital and call me back. I'm on my way to the airport and will get the next flight. Please call me back right away!" Mark's body was shaking. He could hardly take his computer from his desk and slide it into his briefcase.

Back in the conference room, Sean and the team agreed they couldn't let Mark fly home alone on a commercial flight. Lisa said that her firm had access to a fractional jet service and would try to arrange to get Mark a private flight home. From her cell phone she called her assistant to try to set it up. Sean ran out of the conference room and hurried down the hall into Mark's office. Everyone in the entire office now knew something had gone incredibly wrong. They saw the running in and out of the conference room, Alexa crying, and now Mark looking pale and obviously in distress.

Lisa now ran out of the conference room to join Mark and Sean in Mark's office and said, "It's all arranged. Let's get Mark to Teterboro Airport in New Jersey. We have a private plane that will be there to get Mark back to Chicago."

Teterboro Airport in New Jersey is approximately fifteen minutes west of New York City. Mark, Lisa, and Sean together ran out of the office to the elevator in the hallway and came out onto Park Avenue and 34th Street where an Uber waited for them. They all jumped into the black GMC SUV and raced to the airport. No one said a word on the ride to Teterboro except, from time to time, Mark was heard saying softly to himself, "Please God, please let them be all right."

CHAPTER 8

Seven years later – Five days after Father Mark's Easter Sermon

Father Mark decides to take a short trip from his hometown of Ocean Crest to get away to some new surroundings. He's in Cape May, New Jersey, a wonderful beach town with streets lined with bed & breakfast inns. Cape May sits at the southern tip of New Jersey. Each inn is more colorful and statelier than the previous one. All are meticulously kept and beautifully landscaped. The town is very quiet this time of year. It is primarily a summer destination where families and friends gather to enjoy the sea, great food, and fun. Entertainment is everywhere in Cape May from the boardwalk food stands, amusement rides, to the many premier restaurants. This small town has some of the best restaurants along the New Jersey Shore.

As Father Mark sits on the couch in his room at the Sea Gate Inn, he prays. Around him is a Victorian room designed with pale blue colors. The queen bed has a magnificent lace bedspread that hugs each corner. The large headboard and bedpost are in silver metal. Hanging above the bed is a small but exquisite chandelier fashioning five lights. Father Mark is very comfortable here.

He is leaning forward as he sits on the couch with his elbows on his knees and hands folded, his chin resting on his folded hands. Eyes closed, he is thinking and praying deeply. He has been in this position for twenty minutes, almost in a meditative state.

He then speaks softly aloud, praying, "Dear Father in Heaven, use me as your instrument and have me play the music with my words that others need to hear to inspire them and make this a better world to live in. If I have acted in violation of your will, I am deeply sorry. At times, I feel haunted by these thoughts of change, so I need your guidance. In the name of Jesus Christ, I thank you."

He opens his eyes slowly, very slowly, and takes a deep cleansing breath. Father Mark slaps his hands on his knees to say, "Okay, time to get moving." He stands up and goes over to the bathroom to wash his face. He speaks out loud to himself, "Get moving. Where am I going? I came here to think and pray."

Just then, his cell phone rings. It is sitting on the nightstand next to his Bible. He picks it up and doesn't recognize the number calling him. He says aloud, "I wonder if this is another caller to condemn or praise me." Not wanting to answer it, he puts it down, but then something tells him to answer the call. He picks up the phone and slides the lighted bar on the bottom of his iPhone screen to the right. "Hello?"

He hears a deep male voice saying, "Father Mark, this is Jonathan Crew with the New Jersey *Star Ledger*."

Father Mark interrupts and says, "Ah yes, I know who you are. You're the writer who made me famous!"

Jonathan responds, "Father, respectfully, your words made you famous. I'm just the one who promoted them. I have to say, your homily was the most stimulating I've heard in a long, long time. Whether one agrees or disagrees with your influence, I don't imagine many will disagree that it had a stimulating effect."

"Well, I will take that as a compliment. What can I do for you Mr. Crew?"

"Oh, Father, please, it's Jonathan. I'm calling you to see if I could have the opportunity to meet with you and talk."

Father Mark responds, "You mean to write another story, correct?"

"Well, that is what I do and you certainly have a story to tell, maybe the most important story in many years."

Father Mark busts into a genuine laugh, "Now, now, let's not sensationalize my rant on creating happiness and peace. All I'm trying to do is create peace one day at a time. You know Mr. Crew, I mean Jonathan, I'm not sure writing a story is the right thing for me right now. I'm doing some soul-searching, and the last thing my superiors will want is to read a story with me promoting my philosophies."

Jonathan suggests, "Father, let me say this: your words truly touched me. I sat during your homily and felt uplifted and inspired. You said things that I long wondered if the leaders of the Catholic Church ever thought about. You gave me hope that maybe someone can address the needed changes. Here is my request—can we meet and talk? I would love to hear more of your perspectives on spirituality. And I promise you that unless you tell me to print what we discussed; you have my word in the name of God that I will not print it. It would be an honor just to spend time with you."

As Father Mark is listening to Jonathan's appeal, he strolls to the window of his room. Peering out, he can see the south side of the ocean. It is a very calm day and the ocean is flat, like a lake. He smiles at the beauty and how peaceful the ocean makes him feel. "Ah, what the hell, I'm happy to talk with you. Let it be on your soul if you violate your promise in the name of God."

"Great!" responds Jonathan. "How about I come to your office tomorrow morning?"

Father Mark advises, "I'm not there. I wanted to get away for a few days, I'm in Cape May."

"Okay," Jonathan says. "I love it there. I'll come and see you there."

Father Mark laughs softly, "Well, we have something else in common. Okay, meet me at the Sea Gate Inn. That's where I'm staying. How is noon? Will that give you enough time to get all the way down here?"

Jonathan responds with excitement in his voice. "Perfect, and lunch will be on me."

The following day Jonathan arrives just before noon and walks up the freshly stained wooden front steps of the Sea Gate Inn. After the final step up, he arrives on the beautiful wraparound porch that is furnished with white wooden rocking chairs, wicker couches, and glass-topped tables. He pauses to look around at the lovely porch and then looks beyond the porch toward the ocean to get a glimpse of the beautiful blue sea. Today is especially sunny and clear. The reflection of the sun on the ocean waves is enough to make this trip worthwhile.

As he drifts off in his mind, hypnotized by the ocean view, he's interrupted by the voice of Father Mark. "You must be Mr. Crew."

35

Jonathan turns his head to the right and sees Father Mark walking towards him with his right hand reaching to greet him. As they shake hands, Jonathan says, "I thought I suggested it's Jonathan. No need to call me Mr. Crew. Father Mark, it's a great pleasure to meet you." Jonathan is taken aback by the firm handshake of Father Mark. He can feel the positive vibration extending from Father Mark's hand into his own and through his body. They lock eyes and both smile. Father Mark releases his hand and begins to walk down the porch steps as he says, "It's a BEAUTIFUL day," emphasizing the word beautiful. "Let's enjoy this day and walk to the boardwalk and take in God's sea."

Jonathan follows. They come to a boardwalk gazebo that has a wooden bench around the inside parameter. They both look out to the ocean and stay silent for almost a minute, impressed by the vastness of the sea.

Father Mark remarks, "God's beautiful work. The power of the sea is soothing. Where I live, there are benches along the boardwalk. Each has a silver plate attached to the top of the bench with a saying or dedication to someone who has passed on from this life. My favorite one says: *The sea will soothe a troubled soul or lift a joyful spirit even higher.* It is so true. You just need to sit and look out at the sea for a few minutes and your troubles will feel so much smaller, or you will feel even greater than you did when you arrived. We are so lucky to live so close to the sea."

As Father Mark sits on the bench inside the gazebo, he points to the area next to him to suggest that Jonathan sit beside him. "So, let's chat. What do you want to talk about?"

Jonathan sits beside him and takes out his digital recorder. "I'll record our conversation, and if you want it deleted after we talk, we'll delete it."

"Fair enough," agrees Father Mark.

"So, what inspired you, Father, to give that Easter Sunday homily?"

That is all the prodding Father Mark needed, and he began to explain. "You know, the truth is that my frustration has been building for several years. I have discontent for how we, as the Church, lead people. It has gotten to a point where I have trouble sleeping, and I suspect the timing just happened to be right that Easter morning. I wanted to provide a different point of view—that the human spirit is powerful, and that God gave us the power to do great things.

"Jesus taught us that we can do even greater things than he did. He instructed that God is in us and there is a better way to live. God sent Jesus to us to teach us how to live better, to help us understand we can be born again while we live, and that when we pass from this life, there is an even greater place for us. As a Church, I don't feel we teach this well enough, and I want to inspire change."

Father Mark pauses for a few seconds and then begins again. "Unfortunately, life gets in the way sometimes. We all experience all kinds of pressures—family pressures, work pressures, or relationship pressures. We are bombarded by the negative news every day, and we stop being childlike. Jesus told us that to enter the kingdom of heaven we must be like children. What I think he meant is we must be limitless in our thinking—free and happy.

"But, at times, life brings us down. We forget that we are all powerful, and that we can achieve great things if we follow the right principles. We can be truly happy if we have the right perspective on things that are going on around us. If we don't see life's challenges as reasons to be down and negative but rather understand that the challenges we face are part of the journey, we will all be happier and more successful.

"If we see the challenges as a learning experience, we understand they are necessary for a successful life. If we understand that God's peace is with us and all we have to do is be quiet in our mind a few times a day and talk to God, great things will happen. The law of positive expectancy will bring the power of the Universe and God to us for true happiness.

"I believe that the Catholic Church can do more to teach us about these things. While I understand the power and beauty of the Catholic Mass, I don't feel we are giving our congregation their money's worth. We go through the tradition of Mass day after day, week after week, month after month, and year after year. But what do the people attending Mass really get out of it? Have you ever taken inventory of the attendees in Mass in most of our churches? The youth is disappearing. Most people appear to daydream, and I believe 70% to 80% of the attendees are there because of obligation.

"Obligation! Is that what we want our followers to feel? Or do we want them to feel enlightenment? You know, Jonathan, if we combine the power of God with the power of our minds, there isn't anything we can't do. If it's in our desire to do it, to ask God for help, to use the power of our minds, and, of course, to work hard and be willing to pay the price for success, we can do great things."

As Father Mark continues, he stares out at the ocean. "So, during my Easter homily I wanted to communicate that we need to change. The Church has the power to do so much more. We need to teach the people that they can live great lives and get through all the problems that will inevitably come their way."

Father Mark pauses and points out to the ocean and says, "Look out there. Dolphins!"

"Where?" Jonathan asks with excitement.

"There!" exclaims Father Mark pointing slightly to the right of both of them out toward the ocean. While Father Mark keeps his arm outstretched and pointing, they see a school of dolphins raise up and then down into the water, as if in concert to music. Their graceful forms glide so easily in and out of the water. Father Mark then says, "God made many great things. How beautiful."

Jonathan nods his head in agreement but stays silent. He then asks, "Father, where do you see the Church in the next ten or twenty years?"

"That is a very interesting question, Jonathan. In my opinion, if we stay the current course, we will lose many followers, financial pressure will get stronger and, who knows, many of the churches could close like many of our Catholic grade schools have.

"You know Jonathan, I often like to read business books. They teach me a great deal. One in particular is by Jim Collins, and it's called *How The Mighty Fall*. In this book, he writes several case studies of corporations that were once the best of the best, big profitable firms delivering GREAT value to their customers." As he says this, Father Mark spreads his arms out wide above his head to demonstrate the size.

He continues, "But then they lost their way. How, you may ask? By becoming arrogant, by believing they are too big to fail, by not listening to their customers and how their needs are changing. The book is fascinating, and I believe every businessperson should read it."

Father Mark stands up to make a direct point. The volume of his voice rises. "You know who else should read it? The leaders of the Catholic Church, right up to those in the Vatican. You see," and Father Mark points at Jonathan, "this mighty institution is failing. We are arrogant, and we live by old rules."

Father Mark paces inside the gazebo as he continues making his points. "We are not listening to the teenagers and what they need, and we are not listening to the elderly and what they need. We have shameful sex scandals, and we hide behind financial payouts. We are an old, stodgy company that is slowly going out of business. But we CAN BE," he adds, and emphasizes those two words, "a great institution that continues to grow and serve the people the way they need to be served. The Catholic Church is, and has been, a great institution. But we need to get back on course, or we can be another example of a great institution becoming minimized."

Jonathan sits listening attentively with his recorder on the bench. "So, you actually think the Catholic Church could disappear?"

Father Mark walks to the gazebo railing and grabs it with both hands, his back to Jonathan, and leans forward. He peers out trying to get a closer look at the ocean. "Like any other organization, if you stop delivering value, you'll go away. It may never totally happen, but we can go away in the minds of the people."

"So, how do we stop that from happening?" interjects Jonathan.

Father Mark turns around and looks back at him, then smiles, "I think we start by touching everyone's heart and guiding them to understand they can live a happy and successful life. We need to teach them how to use God's power to set and achieve their goals, whatever they may be, to teach them that there are principles to follow for a successful life, and teach them to meditate and visualize what they want, just as Jesus taught us. We need to have them understand that God has a great plan for them, and all they need to do is ask God for help.

"Let me tell you a story, Jonathan." As he says this, Father Mark draws close to Jonathan, almost sitting on the recorder. Jonathan picks up the re-

39

corder and holds it. Father Mark continues. "Several years ago, I counseled a young woman who had been married only a few years and had a very difficult relationship. It was one of those situations where she got married young to a long-term boyfriend.

"As they grew a bit more mature and older, she felt very different. While she cared greatly for him, she knew she didn't want to be married to him any longer. Basically, they grew apart. She got lots of pressure from her family to stay in the marriage. Lots of guilt came her way—lots of Catholic guilt. She came to me for help, and we met several times.

"After a few meetings, I told her that God loves her. God will always love her. God would love her if she remained married or got a divorce. God wants her to be happy. I told her she shouldn't live her life for anyone but herself. She needed to follow her heart. While she did that, I asked her to follow Christian principles and do the right thing, and to do the hard things respectfully. If she did that, she would experience short-term pain but, in time, God would see to it that she would be happy.

"Then I made one recommendation. I asked her to go think for a week or so if she should really give this marriage a fair try and, if she gave it one more try, she should not do it for anyone else but for her own soul. If she ended it now, would she feel she really gave it all she could? I reminded her that she wanted no regrets. She came back to me a few weeks later sharing the news that she decided to give her marriage one more try. Then, several months later, she returned and informed me that she decided to end the marriage. She thanked me for guiding her and loving her, and for not giving her any guilt.

"That, Jonathan, is one small example of what we need to do for our people. You know, the Church rules state that she can't receive communion now that she's remarried ... unless she gets an annulment. You know, I don't agree. She loves God and respects being a Christian. Why should we turn our back on her? You know what I mean?"

Jonathan nods in agreement. "Yes, I sure do. During your Easter homily, you said you believe anyone should be welcomed to receive the host during Mass, not just Catholics."

Father Mark reaffirms, "As I said that morning, if it really is the body of Christ, why would we not want everyone to have it."

Jonathan stands up and strolls slowly around the gazebo. "Yes, I couldn't agree more. But I'm not sure many other Catholics would agree."

"I think you'd be surprised," Father Mark responded. "They may be afraid to admit it, but I think many would agree."

Father Mark then stands abruptly. "I'm hungry. Let's go get some lunch." The two exit the gazebo and walk back toward the Sea Gate Inn.

As Father Mark and Jonathan sit at a table for four in the dining room, giving them ample room, a waitress comes by and pours them some water. She asks, "May I get you anything else to drink, gentlemen?"

Father Mark politely waits for Jonathan to respond first. "May I have a club soda with a splash of Diet Coke please … oh … and a lime?"

The waitress looks puzzled but writes it down on her order pad and Father Mark looks at Jonathan in amazement. "I can't believe you ordered that. That is my favorite drink. Make that two," Father Mark says this without moving his eyes from Jonathan. The waitress giggles and walks away writing "2" on her pad. With a bit of surprise, Father Mark says, "Well, I guess we've been divinely connected! I don't know many people who order this drink. No, actually, I don't know ANYONE who orders that."

Jonathan laughs, "Me neither. My wife makes fun of me about this drink, so now I can tell her that divine guidance put it in my head." They both laugh at this.

"I like your vibe, Jonathan. There is something special about you! I think you're going to write a very good story. One thing I ask, please don't interpret our discussion too much. Keep it as factual as you can. I don't want to have a situation where your words and thoughts dominate the story. Let my words be the story." Then Father Mark mumbles, "Even though I may regret this."

Jonathan turns the recorder back on. "If you could recommend just one thing that people do to improve their lives, what would it be?"

Father Mark likes this question. "That is an easy one—pray more!"

"Okay, and outside of praying?"

"Okay" Father Mark continues, "stop gossip and negative talk. Control your thoughts. The power of thought is the most powerful thing we have."

Gossip is an epidemic. Where do children learn to gossip and be negative? From their parents. Imagine the impact on children at the dinner table when they hear their parents complain about their friends, their work, or their co-workers. How they talk about the clothes other people wear, how their children's coaches aren't being fair, or how teachers are too difficult. It's like the negative news on TV, everything is negative and critical. We all know about the cyber bullying that goes on and how negative social media can be. If people would just try to shift the tone of their speech and talk in a positive way, look at the positive in others, and not judge.

"A very wise person said, '*Thou shall not judge.*' Use words of encouragement. This would have a profound positive impact on the world. This is what is meant when Jesus said, '*Love one another as I have loved you.*' He didn't say, '*Go and gossip and rip each other apart.*' So, there's your answer. If we all do that, if we all do it for one day of our lives, we could have a single day of peace!"

Jonathan then asks, "Can you go back to the point you made about controlling the thoughts you think?"

"Sure, what do you want to know about that?"

Jonathan pauses and then, somewhat confused, says, "Don't we all control our thoughts?"

"Here's how it works, Jonathan. We all have between 60,000 and 80,000 thoughts going through our minds on a daily basis. If we wrote down all the thoughts as we think them, and at the end of the day go back and reviewed them, we probably would be amazed at what we are thinking about all day long.

"Most people have a negative slant to most of their thinking. They think things like, *I'm too skinny, I'm too fat, I'm not smart enough, I'll never be able to buy that, I don't know how to get my kids to listen to me, it's the Republicans' fault, it's the Democrats' fault,* or *I hope I don't lose my luggage on this flight.* The more they think the negative slant, the more of it comes true.

"Life is a self-fulfilling prophecy in that what we think about and believe we create. We attract from the Universe and from God that which we put out there. So, if we as Catholics, as a spiritual entity, teach people how to identify negative thoughts, push them away, and replace them with *possibility* thoughts, we would create an amazing positive energy.

"Let me tell you something you may not be aware of. It's a true demonstration of the power of thought and words, and how thoughts are real vibrations that impact everything around us. Did you know our thoughts and words can positively or negatively impact water?"

"Water?" questions Jonathan with confusion.

"Yes. When you get home, look up Dr. Masaru Emoto and watch some of his YouTube videos. He did experiments where he put water under very strong microscopes and examined the state of the crystals inside of the water. When he and others who conducted the experiments with him used negative words, the water crystals became ugly. When he prayed or used positive words, the water crystals became beautiful. It's fascinating. Go check it out. He did so many amazing experiments that prove words and thoughts have power and energy. Make sense?"

"Yes, it does. That's amazing. I'll certainly look into that. But controlling your thoughts isn't easy to do."

"That's true." Father Mark raises his voice and says, "BUT, if you commit to doing it one day at time, even just one hour at a time, it gets easier and easier every day. Let me give you an example of this in real life."

Father Mark takes out his iPhone. "When Steve Jobs created the iPhone, do you think he told his company things like… awe, this may be too hard to do, we may never be able to make a phone that is a pocket-sized computer. It could cost too much, potentially no one will buy it, and it could easily break." Then, his voice getting louder, he says, "Or did Steve Jobs say all things are possible. Let's change the world! We can do it! Let's keep trying until we get it right, never take a setback as failure, or other determined statements? I wasn't there, but I read enough about him and how he drove his people hard with possibility thinking. He always set positive expectations to create new technology. Look what he created! We can all create an iPhone in our lives if we think and act properly."

Other topics Father Mark and Jonathan discussed included how Father Mark became appalled at how the Catholic Church covered up the child sex abuse scandal, how the Church is losing the millennials, why Father Mark believed that women should be priests, and why marriage for priests could be a positive transformation for the Church.

The waitress comes and takes their lunch orders. Father Mark orders a salad with grilled salmon and Jonathan a turkey club sandwich. A few minutes later the waitress returns with their food.

As Jonathan begins to eat his sandwich, he asks in a soft quiet tone, "Can I ask a very personal question?"

"Sure thing," says Father Mark, as he continues to casually eat his salad.

"This won't be part of my story. I'm wondering … I know you were married before you became a priest … what happened to your family and how did you become a priest?"

Father Mark looks up at Jonathan, pauses a few seconds, takes a deep breath, then places his fork on the table and speaks in a serious tone. "There is no way to sugarcoat it, so I'll just say it straight out. My wife and two boys were killed in a horrible auto accident. There wasn't any foul play, no alcohol or drugs involved. The other driver just got distracted and hit my wife's car head on. The other driver didn't survive either."

"Oh my God!" Jonathan gasps, as he places his right hand over his mouth in shock. "I'm so, so sorry. Just so sorry."

Father Mark continues, "I had a board meeting with a company I had just been named CEO of, and I got a call that there had been a terrible accident, and I had to get back to Chicago right away. The worst day of my life!"

"Oh my God! How did you deal with that? How are you such a positive and inspiring person after experiencing such a tragedy?"

Father Mark responds, "Well, as you can imagine, that became a very difficult time in my life. I felt dead inside for about a year. I lost faith in God for a short time, didn't want to see friends, didn't want to work." Then Father Mark raises his voice, "I COULDN'T work. I felt like a zombie. I tried to make sense of it all. I cried, cursed God, prayed to God, asked God for answers and—nothing. No answers. Just grief. Many, many, many, long sleepless nights walking around my townhouse in Chicago.

"I had my family cremated, so I would go into my office in my home and talk to the ashes in the urns. Talk to them as if they were actually there with me. My only sibling, my brother, had passed away many years before, and my parents had passed on after living a great long life, so I didn't have them either. Many nights I thought about suicide. I felt no reason to live, and my mind started to tell me to go to that spiritual place with my wife and children. Of course, it made perfect sense. Why grieve? Why have pain? Just end it and move on to the next world. But, at the same time, I had this small voice inside of me that spoke differently. It told me that I will never do it. There had to be something else for me.

"So, after almost a year of this, I broke down. I remember it being a summer night in July, my family and I always loved the summer, so that time of year was very difficult for me. We hated the cold, so why on Earth did we live in Chicago? Anyway, at about 3 a.m., I felt very lonely, sitting in my office, and I began to seriously consider going into the garage to hang myself. But, again, I knew I wouldn't do it. And I got so frustrated that I broke down and cried heavily for almost two hours. I never cried like that before. I couldn't control it. Crying and hyperventilating. I cried so hard that my face dripped in tears, and my shirt became drenched. I cried so much into my hands that I must have been running them from my face to my head because my hair became dripping wet.

"Then, I fell to my knees and screamed at God and confessed how sorry I felt for losing my faith. And, while I asked God for guidance thousands of times after my family died, this time felt different. All I can say is that, as I stayed on my knees dripping wet from my tears that formed a small puddle on the hardwood floor, I must have asked more deeply from my heart and soul. All of a sudden, I felt different. I felt light as a feather. I felt this heat leave my body and a sense of calm came over me. I looked around expecting to see someone there but, of course, I remained alone. My heavy crying began to slow down dramatically. I felt clear in my head. I felt relief. Then I got this thought in my mind to take a deep breath, stand up, and stretch.

"So, that's what I did. I stood there and asked out loud, 'Okay, what should I do?' Then into my mind came the thought, *Pick yourself up and help others. Be the person God made you and you always have been. Help the world, and you will feel fulfilled. Be one of God's ambassadors."*

While Father Mark explained this to Jonathan, he looked into his eyes. But now, as if coming out of a trance of deep emotions, he became aware that Jonathan's eyes had accumulated tears. "Oh, Jonathan, I'm so sorry for upsetting you. I didn't mean to do that. I just got carried away. I haven't spoken about this in some time."

As he takes his right hand and wipes away tears in the corner of both eyes, Jonathan responds. "It's okay. Please continue."

Father Mark pauses in silence for about ten seconds with a concerned expression.

"It's okay, really. I want you to continue," repeats Jonathan.

Still looking hesitant, Father Mark continues. "So, I start to walk around my office, like from one end of the room to the other, just pacing. I feel this relief, but I'm still confused. My nose is running from crying, and I'm wiping it with my sleeve with my right forearm."

Father Mark slightly raises his voice, "So, I then say, 'What should I do?' Again, a thought comes in my mind, and it tells me … *Go give someone a single day of peace.* A single day of peace? What does that mean? Then it dawns on me that I'm being guided to help others. Of course! We all know that when we're in pain, the fastest way to relieve it is to do something good for someone else.

"So, I think, okay, today I'm going to go find someone who needs help and make their day better. Just then, I felt the spirit of God in me and around me. I thought of my family, but this time I didn't feel desperation. I felt sad but renewed. It's so hard to explain. The best way for me to describe it is that I felt free.

"So, to make a long story short, for the next few weeks, every day I would go help someone. It started that morning helping a homeless person. I told myself that I would go for a walk and God would show me who to help. I strolled slowly about a half mile. I remember the weather being abnormally cool and breezy for that time of year, but it felt refreshing, like the feeling you have skiing down a mountain with the clean, cool air blowing around you.

A Single Day of Peace

"As I walked from my house into the city, I saw a homeless man sitting comfortably in front of a diner. He sat with his back straight up against the wall, his arms hugged his knees that were raised up about chest high. Not thinking much about it, I sat next to him and started a conversation. He looked at me in surprise. I suspected the seat next to him had been vacant for a long time. He smiled. He appreciated my presence.

"I found him to be an articulate man. He had gotten involved in drugs, lost his job, had no family, and just lived on the streets. He said he never felt lonely because there were many like him. We all have networks, I guess. We talked a bit about sports. He shared that he enjoyed being a lifelong Cubs fan. I asked what he knew about the current political landscape and, surprisingly, he knew exactly the sad state of affairs. His daily ritual included hunting down newspapers thrown into the garbage. He joked that inventory is low these days with digital communication!

"I invited him into the diner for breakfast. He politely declined, because he hadn't had a shower in some time. He didn't want anyone to feel uncomfortable with his uncongenial attire. So, I went in and bought him eggs, pancakes, toast, and coffee. I brought it outside and sat next to him for a bit as he enjoyed his feast.

"When I left him, I realized that for that thirty minutes I felt happiness. I hadn't felt happy since my family's accident. And, on my walk home, I thought about what made me the happiest outside of being with my family. I easily recalled that I felt the most fulfilled during my business career while helping others, coaching them, and mentoring them.

"So, as I walked home, I made a commitment to myself that I would do something for someone else every day. That night, I slept through the entire night—the first time since I lost my family. So, for the next three weeks or so, I helped someone somewhere. I gave them a single day of peace at hospitals, children's hospitals, homeless shelters, seniors' homes, and the homeless on the streets. I even went to animal shelters to help animals. I decided on a mission to give a single day of peace to someone or something every single day. I still missed my family, but life came back into me. I still cried from time to time, but I became different. I didn't feel angry. I wasn't desperate. No bitterness. I felt free.

"Then, within about a month more of doing this, I began thinking about the thoughts I had during my college days, and about how I considered becoming a priest. That thought kept coming to my mind and, one day, while eating a sandwich in my kitchen, I asked God out loud, 'God do you want me to be a priest?' I didn't get a direct answer, but I did think about doing research on it. So, I did, and one thing led to another, and here I am."

Jonathan sits calmly, obviously touched by this story. The next three words drift slowly from his lips in a low tone as if ruminating to himself. "Amazing. Simply amazing." He looks up at Father Mark. "So, during your younger days, you had thoughts of becoming a priest?"

"Yes, I did. I thought about it often. Don't know why. I felt attracted to the idea of being close to God, helping others, and being as spiritual as I could. Now, don't get the wrong idea. It's not that I was a 'holy roller' and talking about God when hanging with my friends. I did some stupid things like most kids do. Got into a little trouble, snuck some alcohol into a party, tried to impress the girls. You know, typical stuff.

"But I always had this little voice inside prompting me to think about making the world a better place. While I had fun as a kid and played sports--I loved baseball the most—I tended to see most things on the spiritual side. For example, when at a baseball field and I saw a mother goose with her goslings, I would say to myself, *there's another indication of God.* Even the goslings follow their parents, and the parents love and take care of their children. I don't know, that's just how I ticked."

With that, the waitress approaches the table. She scratches her cheek, almost self-consciously, and asks softly, "I'm sorry to interrupt you, but can I get you anything else?"

Father Mark looks over at Jonathan and raises his right hand, palm up gesturing towards Jonathan.

"Nothing for me," Jonathan confirms.

Father Mark looks up at the waitress and smiles. "We're ready for the check. Thank you."

A Single Day of Peace

The waitress smiles back and walks to the counter to prepare the check. She returns quickly, but Jonathan doesn't let her put the check on the table and hands her his credit card. "Thank you, we enjoyed a delightful lunch."

As the waitress walks to the front counter to process the payment, Father Mark says, "Thank you, Jonathan. That is very generous of you."

"Not at all. This has been a very pleasurable experience speaking with you, listening to your perspectives, and learning about your life. You are a very special person, Father Mark. You have a way of inspiring people. Today you gave me a single day of peace."

Father Mark stays silent for a moment and then smiles. "I guess that's my calling."

As the waitress brings the credit card slip over to the table, Jonathan signs it, and both stand up. "Thank you, Father. Thank you so, so much. Thank you!"

They embrace in a warm hug and, as they separate, Father Mark looks warmly into Jonathan's eyes. "And you gave me a single day of peace too. Thank you. Now, go write your article and make us both proud."

CHAPTER 9

Father Mark returns from his trip to Cape May and feels refreshed and vibrant. As he sits in his bedroom in the rectory, he thinks about what a difference a few days make when you get away from everyone and everything to think and pray. Over the last three days he strolled the beautiful streets of Cape May, walked along the wide beaches' hard sand near the surf, dined alone, prayed often, and retreated to bed by 9 p.m. every night.

He stayed away from the TV and what he calls "neggie news"—the news channels that promote every negative aspect of what goes on in the world. This allowed him to have clear and clean thinking. During his retreat, through all of the quiet time of thinking, praying, and meditating, he felt even more convinced that he did the right thing by expressing his perspective at the Easter vigil.

Back in his office at the church rectory, he strolls to his desk and turns on his computer to see what his schedule looks like in the coming days. This being Wednesday, he has a few days before he has to be ready for his Sunday 10 a.m. Mass, assuming Monsignor will allow him to conduct it.

As Father Mark scans his schedule over the next few days, he is amazed that he has back-to-back meetings from 8 a.m. to 6 p.m. every day. For every meeting, the church office manager and secretary, Margaret Helms, has inserted the words "personal counseling" in the subject line.

Margaret has been working for the church for nine years and knows every detail about its operations. Father Mark studies the appointments: Michael McDermott—personal counseling, Janice D'Amico—personal counseling, Rick McGreggor—personal counseling, Sharron Riter—personal counseling, and on and on until Friday at 6 p.m. Father Mark recognizes many of the names. Some are young adults between 18 and 23, some are married, and some are elderly.

He walks out of his room and approaches Margaret at her desk. "Marge, my schedule has many more counseling sessions than normal. Do you know what's going on?"

"All I can say, Father, is that the calls came in and I scheduled them. I questioned each of them to confirm they wanted counseling sessions and not just to meet you to express their views on your Easter sermon. They all assured me their interest is counseling."

"All right then. I will counsel."

"Monsignor would like to talk with you at 11 a.m. today. He says he only needs fifteen minutes." Father Mark nods with a smile and walks back to his room.

At 10:55, Father Mark stands outside Monsignor Joseph's office. The office door is open, and the Monsignor is sitting at his desk typing on his computer. Father Mark plans to wait a respectful five minutes. Just then, Monsignor Joseph waves to him to come in. "It's okay, Father. Come on in. Just like you to always be five minutes early."

The Monsignor continues to speak as he stands up from behind his desk and walks around it to a brown leather couch situated to the left. He sits on the couch and Father Mark remains standing. The Monsignor is wearing black jeans and a white golf shirt that expresses the logo of Eagle Trail Golf Club. "Father, I assume you enjoyed your little trip and that you returned with clear thoughts. I don't want to re-hash our views on your Easter sermon, and I would rather move forward to a positive place. As we do that, I just want to know if I should expect any other unconventional perspectives being promoted by you." The Monsignor sits back calmly expecting to hear Father Mark affirm this but, as Father Mark begins to speak, the Monsignor sits up and expresses a disappointed look.

"Monsignor, during my little excursion, I received a call from the writer from the New Jersey Star Ledger who wrote the article about my Easter homily. He wanted to come and meet with me and interview me. Something inside of me told me that I should let him come visit. We met for a few hours and talked. I found him to be very respectful and truly interested in my thoughts."

The Monsignor is now agitated and fidgets in his seat.

"He asked many great questions, and I shared my views. I gave him permission to write an article as long as it reflects my words and not his interpretation. He agreed."

The Monsignor interrupts with a stern voice. "Now we will have even more negative repercussions." He glares at Father Mark. "Mark, this frustrates me. We are here to serve, not condemn the Catholic Church."

"Who says I'm condemning the Church?" retorts Father Mark.

"Your views are not supporting the Church. You are outright disrespecting our long history of doing so much good in the world. Yes, the Catholic Church has made mistakes, big mistakes, but we need people like you to support us. You are a unique priest in that you lived the lay life for a long time and decided to accept the sacrifices of serving others within the Catholic Church. It is healthy to challenge things from time to time, but you cannot go around promoting negative perspectives. I will tell you this, if the article is written and it creates more negative reaction, you should think long and hard as to how you will respond to the bishop."

"I expect no issues," Father Mark responds confidently. "The article will be supporting our institution and express my views on how we can contribute to a more successful and happy society."

The Monsignor looks away reluctantly. "I hope so."

A few hours later, Father Mark receives a phone call on his mobile phone. The caller ID reveals that it's Jonathan Crew. Father Mark had been diligent, adding Jonathan into his contacts. He slides the "accept call" bar on his iPhone from left to right and puts it up to his right ear. "Good day, Jonathan, nice to hear from you."

"It's good to hear your voice, Father. Do you have a minute to speak?"

"Sure," Father Mark acknowledges.

"I just wanted to call and let you know my article is accepted by our publishing staff, and it will go to print for Sunday's issue. Would you like me to send it to you so you can read it in advance?"

"That won't be necessary, I trust you. The fact you called and offered me a preview tells me this will be an accurate reflection of my views. I won't be surprised if it is read by only a few—no reflection on your writing or network of readers."

"On the contrary, Father, it may get the front page, so you could get lots of eyeballs on it!" There is about ten seconds of silence that feels like an hour to Jonathan. "You there, Father?"

"Yes, I'm here. I'll talk to you soon, Jonathan. Thank you so much for the call," and Father Mark presses END.

Jonathan hears three beeps in his ear that signals the call is over. He takes a deep breath and moves the phone from his right hand to his left as he slides it into his left rear pocket.

CHAPTER 10

It is now Sunday morning and the popular Sunday *Star Ledger* has been printed and delivered to homes, grocery stores, delicatessens, newsstands, diners, and coffee shops. The Sunday circulation is over 350,000 and reaches nearby states including New York, Pennsylvania, and Connecticut.

At the bottom right-hand side of the front page is the title *"The Next Generation of Catholic Leaders—My Intimate Conversation with Father Mark Tossi by Jonathan Crew."* Next to the title is a complementary photo of Father Mark. It reveals his full head of jet-black hair, sparkling blue eyes, and a soft smile. The article is an accurate, detailed reflection of the perspective Father Mark gave to Jonathan regarding views of the Church and how it can be more effective in taking an enhanced inspirational role in people's lives.

The 10 a.m. Sunday Mass at St. Jude's Church progresses as any other. But today, the church enjoys a larger crowd than usual. Word has spread about Father Mark, and many enjoy the habit of an early morning read of the Sunday Star Ledger, so they were exposed to Jonathan Crew's article. There is curiosity if there will be further controversial views shared by Father Mark, which prompts a large attendance at today's Mass. After the Gospel is read, Father Mark walks up to the main pulpit located on the right side of the altar and begins his homily.

"In today's Gospel, Jesus tells us to enter through the narrow gate, for wide is the gate and broad is the road that leads to destruction, and many enter through it. But small is the gate and narrow is the road that leads to life, and only a few find it. That leads me to something on my mind."

Monsignor Joseph is assisting with the Mass and is sitting in the right side of the sanctuary in a dark wooden, high-back altar chair. He sits up and quickly moves his unsettled stare from the congregation to Father Mark.

Father Mark continues. "I believe that adversity causes many to go about life trying to find the easy way, the wide gate, and this gets us into trouble. Adversity is something we all face. Whether we are trying to enter the narrow gate or make the mistake of entering through the wide gate, adversity must be overcome if we are going to live a happy and successful life. I want to repeat this: adversity is something we all have to face at some point or at many points in our lives."

Monsignor Joseph is listening very attentively to Father Mark. He is a bit nervous as to where this homily may go and if it will again be controversial.

"Here is what is interesting to me." Father Mark continues. "I do a considerable amount of counseling with people and, as you can imagine, many have issues they are trying to overcome." At this point, Father Mark is stepping down from the pulpit and walking toward the congregation to be more intimate with them.

"Okay, let's have a raise of hands." Father Mark raises his right hand high up. "Raise your hand if you have had, or are having, an adversity to deal with. Come on, raise those hands up." Father Mark is looking onto a sea of hands raised high up. "If you are over five years old and your hand isn't up, then you're dead!"

Laughter rises up from the faithful congregation. "Now, keep those hands up, and look to your left, to your right, behind you, and in front of you. Go on, look around you. Keep looking." Father Mark pauses for fifteen to twenty seconds allowing everyone to gaze around. "Okay. Good. Hands down," and Father Mark lowers his.

"Okay, so what we just did is prove that we all have stuff to deal with. I know, you saw some hands up from people you thought had the perfect life. Yep, they too have or had issues. And you probably saw some people with their arms raised and you were happy to see they have problems!" Many people laugh.

Father Mark is now walking down the center isle looking to his left and right. "So, step one in getting good with your adversities is to realize you are not the only one who has them. When I counsel people, I have to start with this, because part of the anxiety people have is the 'Why is this happening to me?' syndrome.

"It isn't just happening to you. It's happening to everyone. Once you internalize this, you have some relief. You stop blaming God or feeling isolated that something is wrong with you, and that is why you have this adversity. Now you can have a new frame of mind. You can now tell yourself that while you have an adversity to deal with, this is part of life. With no adversity, you are in the graveyard."

Monsignor Joseph relaxes, as he feels that this will not be another controversial homily.

"Okay … now." Father Mark walks toward the front of the church continuing to look right and left as he speaks. "The next step is to pray about your adversity. Ask God and the power of the Universe to guide you through this adversity and show you the way out of it, to guide you to making the right decision, how to act, and plant positive, productive thoughts into your mind. Give it to God, and God will guide you. Then, thank God for accepting your prayer and fulfilling it. When you pray, believe you are free of this adversity, close your eyes and see yourself as happy, healthy, and doing what you love to do without this problem.

"Now comes attitude. Your attitude is what will drive your thinking and behavior." Father Mark reaches the first pew in the front of the church. He turns around to face the congregation. "To improve your attitude regarding this problem, create positive self-talk. Write down some self-talk statements you will repeat over and over. Something like 'Each hour of each day I'm resolving this problem. I am free of it here and now.'" Father Mark crosses his arms above his head, and then separates them quickly as if to waive the problems away. "You may think you are lying to yourself saying you are free of the challenge, but that positive statement puts your mind, body, and spirit into action to get it resolved.

"I also recommend putting a detailed action plan down on paper, or in your computer or, of course, into your smart phone. That's what we all do nowadays, right?" Father Mark pretends to have a phone in his hands using his thumbs to type on an imaginary phone keypad. Many people chuckle.

Father Mark quickly shifts the conversation to a totally unrelated topic. "You know, the other night I saw an interview on TV with the famous rock singer from the band The Who—Roger Daltrey. He said, 'You know what's wrong with everyone today? We all have our heads down. No one is looking up anymore!' I think he's right! By the way, I became a HUGE"—Father Mark stretches out his arms to create the image of *large*— "Who fan during my younger years. See that? Priests love rock & roll too!" More laughter.

"Back to the topic at hand. Make a detailed plan as to how you will attack and rise above the adversity. Again, pray for God's help and energy to execute this plan. Finally, put it into action. NOW, I have always found that when I have adversity, as soon as I get into action to resolve it, I feel so much better. My energy moves from frustration, sadness, and anger to action and productive feelings. It really works! So, get active, get moving, and execute your plan.

"Show me someone happy and successful, and I'll show you someone who has been knocked down by adversity and gotten up, dusted themselves off, and plowed forward. Then they transformed into a stronger and happier person. So, within adversity is the seed to make you better. See it that way and get moving."

Father Mark has now returned to the pulpit, as he concludes his homily with his hands resting on the left and right arms of the pulpit. "Now, I realize some adversities are serious sicknesses, finances, deep relationship issues, and so on. BUT, if you apply this plan to it, you will prevail. I promise." Now Father Mark stretches out his arms with his palms facing the congregation and concludes his homily with, "May God be with you during all your adversities. Invite Him/Her to be there and He/She will be there."

CHAPTER 11

S unday evening arrived and by now the printed and digital versions of the Sunday *Star Ledger* had reached hundreds of thousands of readers in New Jersey, New York, eastern Pennsylvania, and Connecticut. Thousands of readers of the digital version had forwarded Father Mark's article to friends and family around the country. Many posted the link to the article on their social media sites such as Facebook, Twitter, LinkedIn, and Instagram. Before the Sunday midnight hour arrived, over a million people had been exposed to Jonathan Crew's article.

Based on the comments on social media, most of the readers felt inspired by the fresh perspective Father Mark gave regarding the role of the Catholic Church; how irresponsible they were to tolerate and even cover-up the many sexual assaults made on children; how the Church needed to modernize itself and be more of an inspirational source than an institution based on rules, regulations, and ideas that are hundreds and thousands of years old; how the church continues to experience parishioners leaving; how our youth are not attracted to the Catholic Church; and how it is time to be more innovative and change with the times.

One such reader was the very popular late-night talk show host, Jimmy Fallon. Jimmy Fallon is Catholic and, during his youth, he considered becoming a priest. Jonathan Crew's article intrigued Jimmy. He felt encouraged with Father Mark's willingness to be open and somewhat confrontational to the Church.

Jimmy, enjoying the article, went to his computer to do research on Father Mark. He learned that Father Mark had been a very successful businessman, married with children, lost his family in a horrible auto accident, and then became a priest. In searching the Internet further, he read about the Easter homily Father Mark gave and the reactions of significant positive and negative opinions. He read many of the comments and excerpts people posted. He became fascinated with this spiritual personality.

On Monday morning, Father Mark finished his morning run, showered, and arrived in his rectory office. The office manager, Margaret Helms, walked into his office as Father Mark read an email from Monsignor Joseph about arranging a meeting later that day regarding the *Star Ledger* article. "Father, you have a suspicious phone call on hold. The person says he is Jimmy Fallon. I didn't ask him if he is THE Jimmy Fallon, but it certainly sounds like him."

Father Mark looks up from his computer to Margaret and says, "Really? I wonder if someone is playing a hoax. I'll take the call. Should be interesting."

Father Mark reaches over to the phone and presses the blinking line indicating a call on hold. "This is Father Mark."

"Father," says the voice on the other end of the line, "this is Jimmy Fallon, the late-night talk show host, and I read the article about you in the Sunday *Star Ledger*, and I found it very interesting. I wanted to call you to have a conversation. I hope I'm not interrupting you."

"Come on," Father Mark said. "Really? Who's playing a trick on me?"

"No trick, Father. It's me, Jimmy Fallon."

"So, why would Jimmy Fallon be calling me?"

Fallon responded in a serious tone of voice. "Well, like I said, the article about you in the *Star Ledger* caught my attention. You addressed some pressing issues the Catholic Church faces, and I wanted to get more insight from you."

"Well, you do sound like Jimmy Fallon, but I'm sorry to say I don't watch the show very often. Maybe I watched it a few times, so you could be a good impersonator, and I wouldn't know the difference."

Jimmy Fallon chuckled. "What can I do to convince you? How about I give you my office phone number, and you can hang up and call me back? My assistant will answer the phone, and you can ask her. Or, would you like me do a few impersonations to prove it?"

"Well," responded Father Mark, based on an email I'm reading, I could use a few laughs, so how about an impersonation? I'm a Springsteen fan, and I know you do him well. Let me hear Bruce."

With that, Jimmy went into a verse of "Thunder Road."

Within about thirty seconds, Father Mark interrupted and said, "Okay, okay. I believe you. Very entertaining. Thanks for the smile. Now, the big question of the day is what does Jimmy Fallon want to talk to me about?"

"I visited a coffee shop yesterday, and I happened to see the *Star Ledger* at the counter. The headline caught my attention. I started to read the article and immediately became intrigued, so I bought the paper. Nothing against the *Star Ledger*, but I don't recall the last time I purchased it. If ever. I took it home and read the article. Being raised Catholic, I enjoyed your perspective. Frankly, I loved it."

Father Mark jumped in, "You say you were RAISED Catholic? Does that infer you are no longer a Catholic?"

"No, technically, I'm still a Catholic, but I don't actively practice. I mean, I pray, and feel I'm spiritual, but I don't practice, like going to church."

"So, you're like some of the people I spoke about in the article?"

"Yeah, I guess I am."

"Okay, I understand. So, what in particular caught your spirit that made you hunt down my number and call me?"

"After I read the article, I started to look you up on the Internet. I saw you were a businessperson in your past, read about your past life. I'm so sorry for your loss. I read how you became a priest and then about your Easter Sunday sermon last month. Wow! Some people loved your sermon and some felt pretty angry."

"You have to love the Internet," joked Father Mark. "Nothing is private anymore. Yes, I had a life as a businessperson and succeeded in the technology business, so you would think I love the power of the Internet. Well, I do, but privacy is hard to come by. You should know about that Jimmy."

"Oh, I sure do," Jimmy said laughing. "The price of the fame I always wanted. You know, you have to take the good with the bad." Jimmy quickly shifted the conversation. "So, here's my question. Why are things the way they are in the Catholic Church? It appears to be a real mess. As a kid, I loved the Church, enjoyed being an altar boy, thought about becoming a priest."

"Is that true?" interrupted Father Mark.

"It sure is. Then it got too big for me; I don't know. I just didn't feel I should pursue it. Now, with all the scandals, it's hard to be active in the Church."

Father Mark interrupted again with enthusiasm, "Let me say this. The Catholic Church is a massive institution, and sometimes the good we do gets lost. There is no question that we have lost our way. We are not, as a whole, doing enough to inspire people. But, that said, there are many people around the world who are doing great things in the name of the Catholic Church. Catholic charities do wonderful things in helping the poor and needy. Many Catholics are inspiring children, being great leaders, doing what Jesus did. Let's not forget that."

"I understand," Jimmy responded, "but it feels to me that the Church needs to reinvent itself."

Father Mark interrupted again. "REINVENT is a very good word. Yes, I would say we, as a Church, do need to reinvent ourselves. As I have a business background, I often see things through that lens. I see the Catholic Church as a big corporation that lost its way. We all know of major global corporations that once dominated their markets, had a loyal customer base, great products that delivered unique value, earnings grew, and enjoyed handsome profits. Then they got lazy, and believed they were unstoppable. Hubris set in. They got overconfident, cut corners, leaders had scandals, and one day they woke up to find some other company breathing down their neck.

"Before they knew it, they missed their earnings numbers, products got recalled, and then their products became outdated, because the competition out- innovated them. Boom, just like that, they are fighting for their lives. I feel the Catholic Church is much like that, and unless we reinvent ourselves--your word Jimmy—we are in real trouble. That means society is in real trouble, because if we're not here in a powerful way serving men, women, and children, they're not becoming as great as they can be. Me and my fellow church leaders have the power to help people get out of poverty, commit to an education, set goals, dream big, and achieve great things. If we don't do that, everyone loses!"

"Wow!" is the enthusiastic response Father Mark receives. Jimmy pauses for a few seconds, then says equally enthusiastically, "I love your perspective. We need to get you a stronger voice and have more people hear and support you."

"Well, Jimmy, I'm not sure what percent of the people would support me versus condemn me! Not everyone appreciates my views."

Jimmy had a confident tone. "Well, maybe we'll find out. Is it okay if I call you back in a few days? I have to run now and get ready for my show taping, but I would love to pick this conversation back up very soon. I'm really appreciative of you taking the time to speak with me."

"Of course, Jimmy. Good luck with your show, and God bless you," concluded Father Mark.

"And, God bless you too, Father Mark."

With that, Father Mark hung up the phone. He thought to himself, *That's interesting, I have a TV star with a great sense of humor as a new friend. Let's see if he calls back.*

Later that day, Father Mark met with Monsignor Joseph, both in civilian clothes. Father Mark is wearing a blue golf shirt, tan khaki pants, and black running sneakers. The Monsignor wears his typical button-down white shirt and black dress pants accompanied by tan sandals.

"Mark," Monsignor says as Father Mark walks into his office, "come sit here on the couch across from me."

As Father Mark walks towards the couch, he says, "Okay, my spider senses tell me this is going to be a serious conversation."

The Monsignor says pointedly, "I read the Sunday *Star Ledger* article and, while being very well written by that writer, Jonathan Crew, it did cover topics on the edge."

"Yes, Jonathan did a great job, and he did as he promised. He promised to write the article in my words and not interpret or alter them. He's a man of his word. What do you mean by your comment that it covered topics on the edge?"

"Let's face it, Mark," the Monsignor had a polite but serious tone, "you're not a conventional priest. You see things differently from most priests. You have ideals that are different and, in some ways, you see our role as priests much differently than most. Your experience in business and living a civilian life clearly impacts your views."

"Is that a problem?" Father Mark questions.

The Monsignor takes a deep, audible breath, and Father Mark hears his slow, steady exhale. "I just don't know. On the surface, most of what you say makes total sense. It feels right, but it's not the conventional approach, and that makes so many people uncomfortable."

"Please, let's pause right there." Father Mark displays frustration. "Think about what you just said. Isn't that the way greatness starts? Someone thinks differently. They think of the art of the possible and then commit to it, commit to change for the better. They make whatever they touch better. I call that spiritual leadership."

"Or," the Monsignor disagrees, "they are radical and do damage."

"Come on, Monsignor." Father Mark stands up walks behind the couch, pacing while focused directly on the Monsignor. "Don't tell me our people are saying I'm radical?"

"Some are. Some are wondering what your personal agenda is. Why are you creating a stink about things and making it difficult for others? Many people outside of the Church are starting to chatter about you and your beliefs to the point where it feels as if they're asking us all to be more like you. Now, I know you're not radical, that you mean well, and that you and want to change things for the better. But I'm asking you to slow down and stay below the radar. No more newspaper articles. No more controversial homilies. Just be standard for a while."

"Standard? I have never accepted STANDARD. I always want to go way beyond STANDARD." Father Mark's frustration increases.

Before Father Mark can say anything else, the Monsignor interjects. "That's it for now. Please do as I ask. Now, I'm going to go outside on this glorious sunny day, walk the boardwalk, and pray."

Father Mark just turns and walks out of the Monsignor's office somewhat briskly. He returns to his office, sits in the chair behind his desk and presses his hands together in an obvious display of tension. Speaking to himself out loud, he mutters, "Now that's interesting. I'm trying to change things for the good, AND I know I'm doing the right thing, but I'm being asked to be STANDARD. Right there," and Father Mark slaps his right hand down on the arm of the chair, "THAT is what's wrong with our Church."

As he sits silently thinking about what just transpired, Margaret steps in and says, "See that blinking light on your phone?"

Father Mark looks to his right on the desk where his telephone sits and sees line 2 blinking. "Yes, what about it?"

"It's Mr. Fallon again." Margaret walks out and quietly closes the door behind her.

Father Mark lifts the phone, presses the button, and puts the phone to his ear. "Hello, Mr. Fallon. Twice in one day?"

"Hello, Father Mark, and please don't call me Mr. Fallon, call me Jimmy, all the time, please. How has the rest of your day gone?"

"Well, not quite as I would have scripted it. But there is still some day left to make it better."

"Okay, maybe the *better* starts now," Jimmy says with a laugh. "I have a proposition for you."

Father Mark interrupts, "Should I be sitting down?"

Again, laughter from Jimmy. "You're probably already sitting down, but no need to if you're not. I know I said I needed a few days to get back to you but, after our call this morning, I felt pretty excited and approached our executives about the idea of you being a guest on my show."

After thinking for a few seconds, Father Mark questions Jimmy. "Why would you want me, a priest, to be on your show?"

Jimmy responds, "Because you have a fresh perspective as to what spiritual leaders should be doing. You have a unique perspective for a spiritual leader, and I'm confident my audience will connect with it. They will be inspired by you. You will help them see that there are spiritual leaders who are progressive and can be a great inspiration. You would be great."

"I'm flattered," Father Mark says with a smile. "But, I'm not so sure. I've never been on TV before." Then, thinking about what Monsignor Joseph asked of him just five minutes ago, he adds, "And that would not be STANDARD of a priest to go on TV with progressive views."

"Standard?" Jimmy sounds confused. "What does that mean?"

"Inside joke," Father Mark responds.

"Here's what happens. There's a team of people here who will have to vet you. I mean, they research you, talk to you, you know, just to be sure this will go well. Nothing crazy, just to verify what I told them—that you would be a compelling guest. And, if they approve you, and I know they will, then you decide if you don't want to do it—no obligation. It's totally up to you. But, I will say this, you'll be fantastic! The world will love your message. Isn't that why you joined the priesthood, to influence the masses and make this world a better place? I'm giving you a platform to do that."

"Jimmy, that's a very interesting proposition. I'll give it some thought." In his mind, Father Mark quickly concludes that Jimmy made a great point. It's an opportunity to communicate his message and his view on how spiritual leaders can do better, especially Catholic leaders.

"Okay, very well," Jimmy says. "As you're thinking about it, is it okay if I have my team reach out to you and do their thing? It won't take too much of your time. I promise. From there, you can decide what you want to do."

"Okay, Jimmy. Thank you. I hope I won't come to regret this."

CHAPTER 12

Three weeks later on a beautiful Tuesday morning in the second week of May, summer arrives early in Ocean Crest, New Jersey. Being a beach town, summer brings with it a large group of seasonal visitors.

At 9 a.m. Father Mark walks into Monsignor Joseph's office for their scheduled meeting which Father Mark had arranged a few days before. The Monsignor sits in his office chair. "Good morning, Mark!" his enthusiastic voice bounces off his office walls. "Isn't it beautiful out today? I love an early summer. Just love it."

Before Father Mark has the chance to respond, the Monsignor continues, as he looks closely at Father Mark. "I want to thank you for how you've been supporting my recommendations. You've been great, stayed away from controversy, been delivering inspiring sermons, and everyone appears to be pleased with you. Thank you. I really appreciate your support."

After a deep exhale, Father Mark speaks. "Well, Monsignor, you may not feel this way after I explain something."

The Monsignor had bent over to tie his black dress shoe. He stops now and looks up over his desk. He fixes a steady gaze on Father Mark. "Go on." The Monsignor then sits back up in his chair and tilts his head to the left indicating he is listening closely.

Father Mark remains standing on the other side of the desk. "In an hour, I'm headed into New York City for a taping of the Jimmy Fallon Show. A few weeks ago, out of the blue, the late-night talk show host called me after he read the *Star Ledger* article. He said he felt inspired by it. He wanted to talk with me about my perspectives on spirituality, how society today needs more spirituality, why fewer of the younger generation are participating in religion, how he once thought of being a priest, and several other topics.

"He is very genuine, and we had a great conversation. Anyway, he felt that I would be a great guest for his show to talk about these things, to share new ideas on how to be closer to God and have a happier and more successful life."

The Monsignor looks pained. "And to say how great it is to be a Catholic and how the Catholic Church is a wonderful institution. Correct?"

"I'm not so sure those topics are on Mr. Fallon's agenda, but I'm happy to share my perspectives of the Catholic Church," responded Father Mark.

"You're POSITIVE ...," as Monsignor Joseph emphasizes the word positive, "... perspectives? Correct, Father?" Not allowing Father Mark to respond, he continues with furrowed eyebrows reflecting tension. "This is crazy Mark. Why didn't you tell me about this sooner? Why are you unloading this on me now?"

"I wanted you to know and candidly, until a few days ago, I didn't really know what I wanted to do. I had been on the fence, so I didn't see any sense in bringing this up to you. It'll be fine. I think Mr. Fallon is correct, Monsignor. It gives me, actually it gives us, the spiritual leaders, a chance to share our word with the world. If he wants to talk about God and helping people, isn't that what we're all about?"

The Monsignor gets up from his office chair and paces around his office. "Mark, all I can tell you is this better not turn into a shit-storm of your views on how the Catholic Church needs to change, adjust, etc. If it does, it will not be good. I want to be very clear about this. I don't want to deal with any negative repercussions from your one-day of TV stardom."

"I understand your concerns," Father Mark says empathetically. "It'll be fine. I see this as an opportunity to promote successful life principles based on spirituality; to share spiritual leadership. That is why I joined the priesthood in the first place, to spread a powerful word to help as many people as I can about how to live a happy and successful life. This will allow me ... allow us ... to reach millions."

The Monsignor stands in silence staring at Father Mark with lips pursed and concerned eyes. Father Mark stays silent as well, looking into the Monsignor's eyes and waiting for his response.

Then, after approximately twenty seconds of silence, he says, "I don't like it. I have a bad feeling about this. The bishop already sent word about your famous Easter Sunday sermon, and the last thing we both need is having him be unhappy with this situation. I just don't like it. Will you consider withdrawing?"

With that question, Father Mark's shoulders droop, and his face shows disappointment. "Please don't ask that. I want to do this, and I don't want you to try to persuade me not to." With that said, Father Mark uses his best salesmanship tactics and walks close to the Monsignor. He extends his hand to shake the Monsignor's in a sign of agreement, and says, "This will be fine. I'm doing God's work."

The Monsignor reluctantly accepts Father Mark's gesture and silently shares a firm handshake. Father Mark notices the Monsignor's handshake is firmer than usual. The message is delivered.

Then, Father Mark states with a bit of sarcasm as he releases the Monsignor's hand, "I'll see you tomorrow morning and tell you all about it. That is, if I'm not found by a great talent agent and he or she doesn't fly me off to Hollywood!" As Father Mark turns to leave, Monsignor Joseph remains silent. He doesn't enjoy Father Mark's humor.

CHAPTER 13

As Father Mark stands outside the doors of 30 Rockefeller Plaza, he does what he often does in New York City. He looks around and takes in all the energy. A feeling of fond memories wash over him as he recalls his many times in NYC as a software executive—the meetings, the clients he served, the many deals he did, the great dinners … and then the sinking feeling of agony enters as he recalls that awful day he got the news about his family's tragedy. It feels as if it is happening all over again. Those same feelings of anguish come over him. They feel so real.

He refocuses his thoughts by saying a prayer to his boys and wife. This time, it is harder to refocus. He almost breaks down and cries. The very thought of his boys and wife weakens his knees.

Then, almost as a sign, an elderly man comes up to him and said, "You're Father Mark, aren't you?"

"Why, yes I am. Do we know each other?"

"No, we don't. But I visited a friend in Ocean Crest, New Jersey this past Easter, and I came to your Easter Mass when you gave that amazing homily. You are very brave to say the things you said. You totally inspired me! I left church that day realizing I hadn't felt that good going to church in a long, long time. Being so moved, I started reading the Bible every night before going to bed. Just a few minutes and it sets my brain, my energy, and my spirit to the right place for a peaceful and happy sleep. I'm very pleased to be able to meet you."

With that, the elderly man put out his hand to shake Father Mark's, and Father Mark smiled and took his hand, replying, "Well, that's very kind of you. That kind of feedback is so important, because my desire is to inspire people, and I'm happy I did that for you."

Then, all of a sudden, a woman passing by bumps into Father Mark from behind and drops two shopping bags full of items she'd purchased at a nearby clothing store. Father Mark turns and reaches down to assist her.

Noticing his priestly clothing, she says, "Oh, Father, I'm so sorry. I just wasn't paying attention."

Father Mark bends over, helps her pick up the items and places them back into her shopping bags. "No worries, my dear. It's fine. Let me help you get everything back in place." Together, they put all the newly purchased clothing back into the bags. She thanks him and continues on.

When Father Mark turns back around, the man had vanished. Only ten or fifteen seconds had passed between the time they shook hands and then helping the woman with her packages. Father Mark looks quickly all around him, but he couldn't locate the man. *Hmm*, thought Father Mark. *That's odd. He was just here. I didn't even get a chance to get his name.*

With that, Father Mark has a completely new emotion within him. He loses the thought and pain of missing his family and is now engrossed in what the man told him. It makes him feel very confident about his appearance on the Jimmy Fallon Show. He feels validated from the gentleman's remarks. *I'm ready for this*, he assures himself. *That man is a godsend!* He then looks up to the bright blue spring sky and quietly says to himself, "Thank you, Almighty One. Thank you."

He takes one more minute to absorb all the great New York City energy before entering the building. Three or four people pass by at a brisk pace, notice Mark is a priest and offer pleasant greetings: "Hello, Father," and "Good day, Father," or a "Good afternoon, Father." He responds to each with a smile and softly says, "Thank you. God bless."

It's almost 3 p.m. as Father Mark finds his way to the elevators, first going to the wrong elevator bank and then being guided by the lobby attendant to go two sections over. That will take him to Studio 6-B where the Jimmy Fallon Show is recorded. As the elevator reaches Studio 6-B, Father Mark exits the elevator into a reception area where a middle-aged man sits behind the reception counter and greets him.

Father Mark introduces himself, hands over his ID for security verification, and explains that today he is a guest on the show. The man picks up the reception phone and dials. "Hi Leslie. I have Father Mark Tossi here, and he says he's a guest for today's show." After a few seconds pass, he says, "Oh … okay. Thank you." He hangs up the phone and looks at Father Mark. "Leslie will be out to get you in a few minutes."

Soon a young lady in her late twenties with black shoulder-length hair, wearing fashionable jeans and a black button-down shirt, comes out to greet him. "I assume you're Father Mark Tossi?"

"That's me in living color!"

"Great! I'm Leslie, and you can come with me so I can show you around." Leslie leads him down a hallway, opens a door to her right, and they walk into the backstage area of a large studio. Several workers hurry around with papers in hand, cameramen are moving cameras to various locations, and set people prepare for the evening's skits. It looks like a hundred people running around but, in reality, is about thirty or forty. Leslie asks, "Can I get you anything to drink? Coffee? Soda? Water?"

"How about a vodka and club soda?" Father Mark asks seriously. Leslie pauses a moment with a surprised look on her face.

Not wanting her to suffer too much from his request, Father Mark adds quickly, "Just kidding. I bet you didn't think a priest would want a cocktail before the show! I'm just messing with you."

Leslie laughs and looks a bit embarrassed, "You would be surprised with the requests I get from guests before the show! Whatever you need, I will do the best I can to get it for you."

"That's very nice of you Leslie. Water will do fine."

"Then water it is," Leslie confirms, as she walked Father Mark toward the kitchen area where various beverages appeared on three stacked shelves inside an enormous refrigerator. "Do you prefer water cold or room temperature?"

"Room temp is fine," Father Mark responds.

"Here you are." Leslie hands Father Mark a bottle of Poland Spring water, and he follows her out of the kitchen.

"Let's walk this way, and I can show you to your dressing room. In a little while the stage manager will come in and explain how everything works.

You'll meet Jimmy before the show. He'll also take you through all the details and make sure you're comfortable."

They walk past several dressing rooms with signs affixed to the doors. The signs read: Guest Dressing Room #1, Guest Dressing Room #2, and so on. As they approach #4, Leslie points to the door. "This one is yours." It's a very spacious room that includes a beautiful wooden desk and several chairs. Off to the left side sits a tan couch with a glass cocktail table in front of it. The room is quite comfortable with ambient lighting and nice, decorative accents. There's a 52-inch Samsung flat screen TV on the wall. A smart phone is in a re-charging pod with multiple adaptors and a connection for playing music through two small speakers on the floor. "Wow!" Father Mark exclaims. "I could live here!"

Leslie laughs. "We just want you to be relaxed and enjoy yourself." Then she points to the far-right corner of the dressing room. "That refrigerator has more water, soda, all kinds of drinks, and snacks. Feel free to help yourself to anything."

"That's very nice of you all to do this. Thank you."

"Now, let me take you down the hall so I can show you the makeup room." They walk down a hallway to a glass-enclosed room that has MAKEUP etched in the glass across the large front-window. Inside the room sit four beautician-style chairs fastened to the floor. Mirrors and lights fill the room. "Now, just down this way is another kitchen area where food will be served shortly. There are all kinds of sandwiches, salads, soups, snacks, the works. Please be sure to get some food before you go on so that you aren't hungry."

"Will do," Father Mark responds. "Can I get a doggie bag to take some food home?" he questions.

"Sure. Why not?" Leslie says.

"Ah, just kidding," quips Father Mark. "By now, you can tell I like to joke around a bit."

Leslie smiles and nods. "Okay, it's almost 3:30, so let's go back to your dressing room so the stage manager can come in and get you ready."

As they enter Father Mark's dressing room, right behind them comes a middle-aged man wearing slim black jeans, a white tee shirt, and black Converse sneakers. "Hey, Father Mark. I'm Stephen Spano, one of the stage managers here, and I want to take you through a few things." They shake hands and take a seat on the couch together.

Leslie says, "I'm going to head out Father Mark. You'll do great. Enjoy the experience!"

"Thank you, Leslie." Father Mark gives her a warm smile then turns his attention to Stephen Spano.

Stephen and Father Mark speak together for a little over thirty minutes as Stephen explained all the things that will go on until approximately 5:05 p.m. when Father Mark will be standing in the wings of the stage waiting to be introduced by Jimmy Fallon. Father Mark is the first guest, followed by a new up-and-coming singer and guitarist, then a comedy skit, and then the guest star of the evening, the great actor Denzel Washington.

"I have to tell you, Stephen, I'm pretty relaxed, like I'm supposed to be here."

"You are supposed to be here," Stephen confirms.

"But this is still all very crazy. How I got here, I don't know."

Stephen gets a serious but pleased look in his eyes and says, "God works in wonderful and, sometimes, strange ways. Tonight is your night, Father. I'll be back in fifteen minutes to take you to makeup to get ready." With that, Stephen stands up, gives the "thumbs up" sign to Father Mark, and begins to leave. Then, just before he gets to the door, he stops abruptly, turns around, and says, "Oh, almost forgot something. Our strict rule: please leave your cell phone here in the dressing room when you come to the stage. We don't want cell phones ringing when you're live!"

"Makes sense to me. All good."

At 5 p.m. Father Mark stands in the wings ready to be cued by another stage manager. Jimmy Fallon is doing his opening monologue and, as usual, he has the crowd warming up very quickly. He jokes about the president, the recent controversial happenings at the NBA playoff game, and jabs fun at current events. He has everyone laughing before concluding and breaking for a commercial.

Since the show is being taped for that night's time slot, no commercials would interrupt the flow. Jimmy walks to a stagehand and gets a bottle of water and takes a long drink. He hands the bottle back and walks over to his main position behind the studio desk. The director gets the signal that Jimmy is ready to continue and raises his hand to quiet the crowd. Simultaneously, an announcement is made: "Please become silent, as the show is continuing." With the audience quiet, the director announces that everyone is ready, and they are proceeding to the next section of the show. "Action in 3, 2, 1 – Action!"

With his big infectious smile, Jimmy speaks to the camera and to the audience. "Okay ... we have a very interesting guest tonight. Kind of an odd guest of sorts. Father Mark Tossi is a Catholic priest from New Jersey, and he has a very unique and novel perspective on religion, God, spirituality, and the Catholic Church. His fame began to grow after he gave a somewhat controversial homily at his church this past Easter Sunday. Then a writer from the New Jersey *Star Ledger* wrote a front-page article about him and his beliefs. I happened to see the article, and I read it. I became immediately intrigued, because his perspective is very different from typical Catholic priests. So, I wanted him on the show to talk about all these things. Please join me in welcoming Father Mark Tossi!"

Father Mark walks onstage with a confident stride and a pleasant, calm smile on his face. The applause has a pleasant and obligatory sound. He approaches Jimmy, they shake hands, and Father Mark takes the seat at the right side of Jimmy's desk. "Okay, Father, let's start with this question. If you can tell this audience, and the many people watching from home, one thing about spirituality, what would it be?"

Father Mark pauses and says, "Well, Jimmy, I would tell everyone a few things. First, God loves them. God loves everyone. And second, God wants you to be all you can be. You can be successful, wealthy, happy, a great parent, a magnificent teacher, an effective server of others ... whatever you want to be. God wants that for you."

Jimmy jumps in and says, "You see, Father, right there, that is a different perspective. Priests always say God loves us, but they don't take it to the point of saying all is possible. That everyone can be great. They don't inspire the personal growth of an individual."

"I agree, Jimmy. I think we, as spiritual leaders, should do a much better job by inspiring everyone to think big and go for it. I call this spiritual leadership. Spiritual leadership is something everyone can benefit from. And by the way, spiritual leadership is not just for priests to display. Corporate executives and employees would benefit greatly from executing these principles as would parents, teachers … anyone.

"Jesus taught us how to pray, and he told us we can have great things in our lives. He taught us many great things, and one of them is 'Whatsoever you desire, when you pray, believe that you have already received it, and you shall have it." He also said, "If you can believe, all things are possible to him who believes.

"What did he mean by these statements?" Father Mark answers his own question. "He meant that we must believe we can achieve what we desire, and we have to meditate when we pray, to use the power of attraction and, most of all, have FAITH, and that positive energy we display will gravitate these things to us. So, if we pray for something, we must visualize ourselves already having it … health, a new job, a new car, a loving relationship … anything. This approach attracts to you the things you want in your life. Unfortunately, too many people think about all the negative things too much, and they attract that to themselves. Life is a self-fulfilling prophecy. We get from life what we ask of it.

"Now, Jimmy, as I share the perspective that all things are possible, we must be careful to discipline ourselves. We must be sure to govern ourselves. If I can be straight with you, Jimmy, your world of entertainment is an example of excess. Excess will drive us to deep unhappiness. So many in the entertainment business have gotten caught up in the syndrome of *more* and lost their soul."

Jimmy nods his head and tilts it to the right showing his approval and engagement in Father Mark's comments. The audience is experiencing an uplifting and eudaemonic feeling from Father Mark's discussion.

"While each of us aspires for progress, we must restrain ourselves. Will the new pool really make you happy if you already have a beautiful home and a beach house? Will a second car bring the self-satisfaction you yearn for? Will a new spouse be the answer? Will another degree make you feel you have arrived? We must have internal power to control our desires. Achieving things is great as long as we have gratitude and we feel a sense of satisfaction. The Catholic religion provides us with principles that intend to keep these external desires in check. We just have to teach these principles more effectively."

Jimmy jumps in and says, "Imagine if you and the rest of the Catholic priests took that one message to the youth of our communities and showed them how to create the life they want for themselves. Unfortunately, many priests took other things to the youth and severely hurt them."

"Yes, I agree," Father Mark nods. "It has been despicable how some priests preyed on children and abused them. Horrible. Just as horrible is the massive cover-up. The cover-up went to the highest levels of the Catholic Church and not enough people have been held accountable. Great organizations are built on high standards. Unfortunately, we lost our standards."

With that, the audience cheers very loudly. Jimmy also claps and then opens up his arms to the crowd as if to say, "Listen to this response!"

"This is a topic that is very important to me," Father Mark continues. "We, in the Catholic Church, are losing our youth. We need to be more attentive to what the youth today want and need. They are dying for guidance, and how wonderful would it be if we spiritual leaders became the people the youth went to with confidence believing that we can help and guide them. Rather than teaching people they should come to church to please God, you should do it to help you succeed in school and in life— with real life issues and not abstractions they can't relate to. That is what the youth want."

Father Mark is very motivated now and speaks with great fervor. "If we start with giving what the youth want, and then tie that instruction to the power of God and how God is in them, then they can tap into that power. Then they will WANT to be closer to God. Rather, what we tend to do is preach that they have to please God, go to church, say prayers, read the Bible, etc. Yes, these things are all very important, but first let's give the youth what they desperately want. Let's teach them how to be great."

Jimmy shifts the direction of the conversation. "Okay, I agree. Let me ask you this: How does your network of priests and Catholic leaders take to your views?"

"Well …." Father Mark looks a bit uncomfortable. "Some embrace it and, of course, some are not happy with my views. Listen, any time someone comes to the table with a fresh perspective, especially in an environment that has thousands of years of history, you're going to face some resistance. That's okay. But my fear is that if we take too long to adjust, we could lose hundreds of thousands of members. Potentially millions. We have to innovate our thinking. We have to be a source of energy that helps people find themselves—young and old—and help them to be genuinely happy and achieve their goals, whatever those goals may be."

"You keep returning to the theme of achievement, helping people get what they want out of life. Is that what you and the Catholic Church are supposed to do?"

"I believe one hundred percent that it is one of the things we should do. Let me explain it this way, Jimmy." Father Mark points to the audience that remains fixated on him. "If everyone here tonight learned how to improve their lives, would they be happier?"

Jimmy responds with "Of course, Father."

"Okay. So … if I can help everyone here become happier, what is better than that? If they are happier, they do more positive things for others, they become more productive and their earnings go up, and they contribute to the economy by saving some of their earned money and spending some. They feel good about themselves, and they do good things for others, creating a flow of positive energy. Then I would have them understand that there is a power inside of them that helped them do all this. That is the power of God. That power is in all of us.

"So, in this approach, instead of focusing on the rules of following God or the rules of our specific religion, we focus on the person or the people: their needs, their motives, what is in it for them. With that, they improve their condition in life and then we help them understand how God helped them do this. Now we have a person who is a deeper follower of God and spirituality."

Jimmy asks, "How do we tap into that power?"

"Like I said before, Jimmy, you tap into it by first picking something you want … set a goal. It can be anything. Then, meditate on it and visualize that you have already received it. Pray on it and ask God to intervene. Do this every day with positive expectancy. Do this along with thanking God for providing the thought to you. The fact that you had the thought is validation that it is possible, because God instructed that thought into you. Welcome the setbacks and understand that God is guiding you, and that the setbacks are part of the process.

"Difficulties are part of everyone's life. As Proverbs taught us, *Lean not on your own understanding*. Be humble. Keep visualizing the positive. Stay away from the negative. For example, do you know how many people have a ritual of waking up, turning on the news, and starting their day with all the negative stories?

"I call it 'neggie' news. Then, at the end of their day, before they go to bed, they watch the news and get fed more negative things. Then, they sleep on it, and their brains and subconscious minds process this negative information all night long. They do this for 20, 30, or 40 years. Do you realize the NEGATIVE effect this has on their views of the world? I believe they are poisoning themselves and they don't realize it. The sensationalism of the negative news is harmful. Why aren't there positive news stations? Or news outlets that cover only positive and inspirational stories?"

"Okay, Father, there are some very difficult topics our society is dealing with these days. I would like your thoughts on some of them. I give you the topic and you give me your perspective." The audience continues to be absorbed in the conversation. "First topic, the wealth gap. There is so much political and media coverage on capitalism and the separation of wealth. What do you think about it and how do we fix it?"

Father Mark responds very confidently. "Education and family values. There are clear statistics that show that children in single-family households with lower education commit more crimes, are prone to abuse drugs, earn less, and just have a more difficult time with life. Family love and parental guidance come first and, right behind it, is getting an education, getting through college. If we, as a global society, focus on these two things, great things happen. Children grow up happier and more productive and make more money. This narrows the wealth gap that truly exists today."

"Second topic," Jimmy begins, as he leans forward and is noticeably very engaged in this conversation. "What is the supreme religion?"

"Shit if I know!" responds Father Mark, and the crowd bursts out in laughter. "Seriously," Father Mark continues, "being raised Catholic, I loved the experience. I have studied many religions and, in my view, they're all great. I know, as Catholic leaders, we're supposed to promote that being Catholic is what gets you to heaven. Of course, I'm being a bit sarcastic here, but my point is that being Catholic is great, but being Catholic isn't the only way to spiritual success.

"In my view, being a Christian is key to happiness and success—following and executing the guidance of Jesus Christ. That said, if you are not a follower of Christ but you follow loving principles, provide positive inspiration to others, help others have a day, week, or a life of peace, THAT is what's important. So, I'm not here to claim any religion is God's chosen religion. Let's just love one another and do the right thing as often as we can."

"What is God? Like, *who* is He?" Jimmy asks in a very pointed way.

"Of course, no one knows for sure," began Father Mark. "I see God as the ultimate energy source. This energy source is in all of us, so God is in all of us. We tend to think of God as a person, the man with long white hair, a long white beard, and wearing a long white robe. That is our human interpretation, because our human brains have a difficult time thinking differently.

"I suggest you look around you and see that there is energy in everything—God's energy. The universal energy exits everywhere. It is in every country, in every city, in the ocean, in the wilderness, in the mountains, in every living person, everywhere. Everything we see, other than nature, began first as an idea that someone created. Think deeply about that. Everything around us started as just an idea a human being had.

"These TV cameras," Father Mark points at the many cameras around the stage, "at one time they didn't exist. Some human had an idea about visually recording things and then figured out how it could work and through trial and error made the first recording. Then we evolved to where we are now. Each evolution of the TV camera also started with an idea—idea energy.

"The chairs we're sitting on at one time didn't exist and now they do, because they started in the form of an idea, and that idea became transformed into a physical thing. Everything around us became transformed from an idea ... houses, cars, golf courses, skyscrapers, yachts, computers, smart phones ... even ideas and theories like laws, mathematics ... EVERYTHING.

"So, the energy that had the wisdom, or the energy that *is* the wisdom is godlike. The magnificent God or god energy created this universe and created us. When he/she created us, he/she put his/her energy into us, and that is why we are capable of creating all these great things, and more.

"So, God isn't a male or female. God is the supreme powerful energy that created a plan for us. That energy wants us to be godlike and use the energy to make our lives great. All we have to do is tap into that energy by recognizing it and deciding to be aware of it. The best way to tap into this energy is to manage your thoughts and tell yourself every day you are connected to the god energy source, and God is working with you every day, every second of every day to help you achieve what you want—to achieve or be the person you want to be.

"So, pray to God. Pray to the god energy and thank him/her for giving you that energy and power and continue to ask and confirm that you have the energy. God is in us and with us every second of every day and you benefit from that energy just by being aware of it. The problem is, most people are *not* aware of it, so they don't use it. It's like having a winning lottery ticket in your pocket, but you don't know it's there, so you don't cash it in!"

"Very interesting, Father. Very interesting. I love how you explained that," Jimmy says thoughtfully. "Here's a tough one for you, Father." Jimmy's facial expression reveals he has a bit of a hard time getting this next question out. "Abortion. This topic is always a sensitive one and a very serious one. We know the Catholic Church's view, but what is YOUR view."

Father Mark pauses and then states softly, "No question, this is a very difficult topic." He hesitates again as he organizes his thoughts in order to communicate himself clearly. "The answer I'm going to give is not going to please many people. Pro-abortion, pro-choice, pro-life, whatever position you have on this topic you are going to have some disagreement with me.

"I feel horrible for anyone who is faced with this decision. My internal view is life is precious and life begins to evolve at conception. I would hate to ever have to be involved in a decision to end that life. I would recommend avoiding ending that life if at all possible. BUT, I do believe there are circumstances where it may be justified and, while it is still a very painful thing to do, we can understand."

This stimulated a mix of applause, whistling, and booing among the audience. In response to this, Jimmy and Father Mark unknowingly speak over each other with Father Mark stating, "I told you there would be many not pleased with my perspective." Jimmy holds up both hands to quiet the crowd and instructs, "Come on, everyone. Let's allow Father to share his ideas." Then he turns to Father Mark. "You are very brave to share this perspective. I agree, this is tremendously complicated to say the least."

"All right," continues Jimmy. "You mention Jesus and Christianity; I assume you believe Jesus is the Son of God."

"I do," Father Mark confirms in a very emphatic tone. "I, like most Catholics, believe that Jesus came to help us to better understand the power of God, to help us learn how to live better and, of course, through his death and resurrection, to teach us our sins are forgiven; that we move from this life to another life when our spirit leaves this body we have." As Father Mark says the word *body*, he puts both hands on his chest to accentuate his body.

"So, here's the thing: if you're not a believer in Jesus Christ and you don't believe that he is the son of God, just consider the things he taught. He taught about love, forgiveness, being generous, thanking God, not judging, how to achieve goals, how to pray … I can go on and on. Just read some of the New Testament and you'll learn what Jesus taught. I'll bet whether you're a Christian or not, you will appreciate the philosophies Jesus stood for. And, not only would you appreciate his philosophies, but I bet you will agree that if you lived by them, you will have a happier and more successful life."

"Okay then, Father," Jimmy says, as he reveals his final topic to discuss. "If Jesus came back to this Earth and walked among us, what would happen? How would he see our world? What message would he deliver?"

"Wow! That's a great question. I love this question. Actually, the interesting thing is I have given much thought to this very same idea." Father Mark nods his head in approval. Again, he pauses to gather his thoughts but this time for about ten seconds, which, for most of the audience, feels like a long and uncomfortable silence. Along with Jimmy Fallon, they wait eagerly for Father Mark's response.

"Here's what I think. First off, I wonder if we would recognize him at first. Someone with such deep spiritually, the Son of God, isn't like you and me. He could easily be discounted as being odd. I believe he would promote the same teachings he did thousands of years ago ... stop the sins you know you are partaking in, repent, love one another, have faith in God, realize you have God inside of you ... all the New Testament teachings."

Father Mark hesitates again, and his facial expression evidences the very serious perspective he's going to share. "I think ... Jesus would walk this land and tell us we're getting it all wrong. He would challenge us. He could very well rock our world, and you know what could happen? I think there's a good chance we would crucify him again. Maybe even the Catholics would crucify him this time."

The audience responds with gasps of shock. Jimmy quickly leans back in his chair with a surprised look on his face, lips separating and eyes wide open.

"I think Jesus would look at what we're doing and what we have done for hundreds of years and tell us we have it all wrong. He could look at the Catholic Church and see all the wealth we have, all the expensive churches, even the Vatican City and tell us to sell it all, to take the billions of dollars and give it all away to those in need. Give it to poor countries. Use it to feed starving people. Put infrastructure in countries that don't have running water or paved roads so they can enjoy these simple pleasures.

"He may challenge us and say, 'If you're really a believer in me, sell it all, and do as I say.' His statements in the New Testament would hold true again today ... 'Sell everything you have and follow me,' as well as, 'It is easier for a camel to walk through the eye of a needle than for a rich man to enter the kingdom of heaven.' Many would agree, and there could be an uproar. Many could protest the ways of the Church. Many would fight harder about all the abuse that has gone on in the Catholic Church."

Father Mark continued, "Then, what would happen? The Catholic Church could say, 'This guy is creating a huge problem for us. We have to get rid of this guy.' I'm not saying we would crucify him on the cross the way the Jewish people did thousands of years ago, but I am saying we could very well be guilty of crucifying him in today's style by criticizing him and justifying our existence and practices in the media. We could get powerful people and politicians to support what the Catholic Church does ... and run the guy out of town. Who knows, maybe Jesus would come back as a woman!" With that, many women in the audience stood up and cheered loudly.

Jimmy notices signals from the director that they had to break for commercials, but Jimmy realizes that this is uncommon ground they are traversing, and he doesn't want to interrupt the momentum; so, he looks at the director and shakes his head slightly to say "no." He encourages Father Mark to continue. "Go on, Father, please continue."

"Well, I probably said too much already. Here's my point. We have to re-evaluate everything we're doing as a people and as a Church. If Jesus came back in any form, man or woman, do we really think he/she would agree with everything that's going on? No way. Absolutely no way! He/she would look at what we're doing in the Catholic Church and hit us hard on some things and tell us we have to change. I suspect we won't like his recommendations. Imagine that. The institution that built itself on the work of Jesus Christ looks for ways to denounce his modern form." With that, Father Mark pauses and smiles.

Jimmy Fallon realized that this is a perfect ending to this interview and responds, "Well, Father, this has been an amazing and uplifting conversation. Thank you so much. We will now break for commercials and be right back." With that announcement, most of the crowd stands up and gives

Father Mark a loud ovation. He smiles, put his hands together in a prayer symbol, places them over his chest and bows slightly as if to say, "Thank you."

As the stagehands come in to refill Jimmy's water and adjust his makeup, a murmur resonates from the crowd. Jimmy stands up and says to Father Mark, "Father, I can't believe you said some of the things you did, but it felt wonderful. I'm lost for words. You're amazing."

"Thank you, Jimmy. I don't really know where all this came from. I just spoke from my heart."

"You spoke from God," Jimmy confirms.

With that, a stage assistant comes to get Father Mark to usher him off-stage. As he walks past the long red curtain, most people from the crowd offer support, but a few shout condemning comments.

Father Mark stops suddenly and walks towards the end of the stage, turns to the crowd, and rises up his hands to ask them to quiet down. As silence draws over the audience, Father Mark says, "I'm one man trying to share a perspective to make us all reflect on ourselves and make us all better. To give each of us maybe one greater day of peace than we have ever had. You don't have to agree with everything, and those that do agree, please respect the other's disagreement. Thank you for listening." Jimmy watches from his desk and smiles as he observes at how Father Mark calms the crowd.

Father Mark then proceeds past the long red drapes and disappears backstage, where many of the employees line the hallway and applaud him. He walks past them with a soft smile of acknowledgement. Once inside his dressing room, he thinks through what just happened. He knows he needs to get back to the rectory as soon as possible. He wants to be securely in bed before the show airs tonight.

CHAPTER 14

It is 6 a.m., and Father Mark decides to stop fighting the inability to sleep. Lying on his back staring at the ceiling, he takes a deep breath. He can see through the small gap under the window shade that a bright sunny morning has arrived. He decides to get out of bed and get into the shower. During the entire night, he had tossed and turned and hadn't gotten more than a few hours of sleep. While he feels at peace with all he spoke about the night before on the Jimmy Fallon Show, he knows there could be harsh pushback from the powers that be within the diocese.

As he begins to enter the shower, he has a change of heart. He speaks out loud to himself, "I need to take a run. It's a beautiful morning and, with such little sleep, I need to get the blood flowing."

With that Father Mark leaves the bathroom and walks to his simple, maple wood dresser. He opens the second drawer from the top, pulls out a pair of running shorts and a tee shirt whose logo "Ocean Crest 5 Mile Run – 2019" promoted an annual local event. He puts on his dark blue, mesh Nike running sneakers with the white "SWOOSH," ties them tightly, and heads down the stairs towards the foyer of the rectory.

As he reaches for the front door handle and opens it to reveal the sun-drenched front yard, he hears the voice of Monsignor Joseph say, "I hope you have a great run. When you get back, we need to talk. Right away. We need to talk about your television debut."

Father Mark respectfully turns to acknowledge the Monsignor, but he has already turned and walked away towards the kitchen. Father Mark pauses for a few seconds and then continues on his way out the front door. He jogs down the front steps, across the lawn, and heads left a few blocks east to the boardwalk along the ocean. Five miles and about forty-five minutes later, he returns to the rectory dripping in well-earned sweat.

He showers quickly, puts on a black golf shirt and blue jeans, and heads over to the Monsignor's office. He turns on his iPhone for the first time since he went to bed last night, and he can't believe the volume of text messages, missed calls, and voice mail notices. No doubt, a result of last night's show.

The Monsignor isn't in his office yet, so Father Mark takes a seat on one of the two side-by-side chairs in front of his desk and begins reading some of his texts. Many are from numbers that he doesn't have in his address book, so no names appear. Some provide strong approval for Father Mark's TV debut saying things like, "Father, I'm so thankful that you said what you did. The Catholic Church needs to change, and your perspective is what they need to follow." Another said, "I've been struggling with my daughter's abortion and for the very first time, I feel relief. Thank you for giving me some peace."

But not all the messages provide support. One reads, "The Catholic traditions and rules are what makes the Church great. Stop being a rebel." One painful text state, "Father, I know you well, and I'm deeply disappointed that you feel the way you do about how the Catholics would treat Jesus if he returned to us. DISGUSTED!"

His attention shifts away from his phone when Monsignor Joseph enters the office. The Monsignor walks quickly to his chair behind the desk and, in a very businesslike manner, begins speaking. "Mark, I'm going to get right to the point. I spoke with the bishop very early this morning, and we are in full agreement that you need to re-think your future as a Catholic priest. As you know, each participant in the Church is an embodiment of the *whole* Catholic Church. As priests, we are to support the principles of the Catholic Church. However, we will not force anyone to follow our principles and beliefs. If they don't believe in or follow them, that is their prerogative. They should then find a spiritual path that fits them better. We feel you should search your mind and soul and decide what to do. Do you really believe you are a Catholic?"

Father Mark responds with, "Yes. But I would say I'm a rebel Catholic. I am committed to the Catholic Church, but I don't agree with some of the things we stand for."

"Yes, that's obvious," retorted the Monsignor. "But you don't have the luxury to be half in and half out. You need to be all in or all out. It's that simple."

The Monsignor continues, "By the looks of the social media reaction, there is no way out of this. There are literally millions of likes, followers, and comments all over Facebook pages, YouTube videos, tweets, you name it. You may have become some kind of household name overnight. Only God knows how long this will last, but right now, you're a huge distraction for the Catholic Church."

Father Mark interrupts, "Isn't there a positive side to this Monsignor? We now have people talking about us. People expressing their views. People engaged in important topics. This is what we need. We don't need to hide and just go with the day-to-day status quo. I'm asking you to consider that the status quo is killing the Catholic Church."

The Monsignor firmly disagrees. "I don't agree. We've been here for over 2,000 years, and I expect to be here for thousands more. ENOUGH of this debate. Here is the conclusion. You are put on paid leave effective immediately. You will not serve Mass. You will not counsel parishioners. You can stay here at our rectory, but you should think about your future. Your situation will be reviewed, and we will determine if you will be put on permanent leave."

"So, this is the way you terminate priests?" questions Father Mark.

"We call it laicization. I think you know that. It is our prerogative to remove a bishop, priest, or deacon from the status of being a member of the clergy."

The Monsignor then stands up, obviously signaling that the meeting is over. "That's it, Mark. I have to get to my day's activities."

Father Mark pauses and, while he wants to continue the conversation, he bites his lip and puts a hand on each knee as if to push off of them to help him stand. With a disappointing look on his face and says, "Okay, Monsignor, I understand. Thank you."

He leaves the Monsignor's office and by now the office manager, Margaret, arrives at her desk. "Margaret," Father Mark begins, "can you please cancel all my counseling meetings for the foreseeable future and don't accept any new ones."

"Yes, Father," Margaret responds. "Monsignor has emailed me early this morning about doing that."

"Very well," replies Father Mark.

Margaret adds in an encouraging tone, "Father, I enjoyed watching last night. You're going to make history. Very good history."

"Thank you, Margaret. That means a lot. But you better not say that too loudly. For the repeating counseling sessions on my schedule, I think there are four or five of them, send them an email and copy me. Tell them I need to reschedule, and I will be in touch with them. I will meet with them privately somewhere and have one final session. Thanks for everything, Margaret."

"For you, Father, any time," Margaret says in a supportive voice.

Father Mark walks up the foyer stairs and into his room and sits at the edge of the bed. He had a busy day scheduled, and now it became totally cleared. He has no idea what to do with himself. Perhaps he could spend the entire day reading all the emails and texts he received, but that doesn't inspire him. He has very little interest in reading any of them. He doesn't want to be distracted by all the opinions.

Then his iPhone begins to ring. He quickly concludes that this call is going to be the first of many he will refuse to answer today. But then he sees the name of Jonathan Crew. Almost relieved to see Jonathan's name, Father Mark answers the call, puts the phone to his right ear, and says, "Jonathan, what a pleasant surprise."

"Father," Jonathan begins, "I can't believe I saw you last night on the Jimmy Fallon Show. Oh …" shifting gears in his talk track "… sorry, Father. Thanks for taking my call. I really appreciate it. I hope you're doing well." Jonathan has nervous energy in his voice, and he speaks more rapidly than usual. He continues, "Okay … Like I said, you were amazing last night. You have no idea how many emails and calls I've gotten because of your appearance on the show last night.

"I suspect your phone is blowing up with calls and messages. You may have inspired millions. You covered topics so many people think about but are afraid to talk about. Sure, some people are not happy with your perspective, but the large majority is so supportive. They just love that you're hitting the key issues head on. The part about the Catholics crucifying Jesus, I don't know what to say but, how you put it, you nailed it. That totally made sense. God, I'm so excited for you. You're going to have media all over you. I'm so sorry, I'm running at the mouth. How are you feeling?"

Not answering Jonathan's question, Father Mark goes in a different direction. "You sound very excited, Jonathan."

"I am. I really am *for you*, because my gut tells me … I don't know … I may be overreacting … but I think you're going to be something like a rock star. What I mean is, people are going to want more from you. They're starving for spiritual leadership, and you're the right person at the right time."

"Truth be told, Jonathan, I always wanted to be a rock star," Father Mark shares a quiet laugh. "Seriously, to answer your question about how I'm feeling, I don't know—a bit numb, shocked, peaceful, and satisfied. Yes, satisfied is a great word for how I feel. I don't know why I feel so satisfied, because just before you called me, I had a meeting with Monsignor Joseph of our parish, and he advised me that I have been put on leave. I can't serve for a while."

"WHAT?" exclaims Jonathan. "How can that be?"

"Well, it seems that my perspective—while it may be inspiring some people—has hit a controversial nerve with our local leaders. I'm frustrated, because if my perspective is putting the Catholic Church in the minds of many, we should use this opportunity to connect with these people, listen to them, find out what their pains are with life and the Catholic Church … then, respond to help them. I really see this as an opportunity to bring people closer to not just the Catholic Church but to being more spiritual, more Christian-like."

"I agree totally," says Jonathan approvingly. "If the Church isn't going to work closely with you and help you minister the people in your way, you should do it on your own."

"What do you mean?"

"What I mean is, you can create a platform to inspire and influence our world. Do speaking engagements, go on TV again, spread the word like Jesus's disciples did."

"Wow! That's a lot to ask for, and I don't know if I'm up to it. Too much is going on too quickly."

"Let me be blunt with you, Father. You have the personality for this. You achieved success as a businessperson before you entered the life of the cloth. You know how to communicate with people. You know how to read people. You know how to lead people. And, most of all, you are very inspirational. Young and old alike gravitate to you, and you can help them transform their lives."

Father Mark interrupts him. "To be honest, Jonathan, I agree. I know I'm very good at these things, and this is why I want to use my talents for God's work. This is why, when I was at a crossroads in my personal life, I wanted to have a spiritual purpose and show people how they can use the power of God and the Holy Spirit that is in them to be what they want to be."

"Exactly," Jonathan affirms. "That's why I'm suggesting you take your word to the people on your own if the Church won't support you. This is exactly what is wrong with the Church. You may even inspire people to change the Church, because if you get the support from the millions that I think you'll get, the Church will not be able to ignore it."

"That's true," Father Mark agrees. "You are now the one doing the inspiring, Jonathan."

"Let me tell you what's going to happen next," Jonathan predicts. "You're going to have the media approach you, maybe even the big networks like CNN, NBC, ABC, Fox … all of them. You're a controversial person right now, and the media loves controversy. They need hot new stories to keep viewership. They'll want to interview you and hear more from you. When they learn that you have been put on leave, they'll want to talk to you all the more. I know someone at the Today Show, and I can see if they want to take what you did on the Jimmy Fallon Show and have you on their show."

"The making of a rock star," jokes Father Mark. "You know, Jonathan, it sounds interesting, but let me digest things for a while. Please don't reach out to anyone just yet. Let me pray on this for a bit."

"Father, can you hold on for a minute? My boss is calling me on the other line."

"Sure, no problem."

As Father Mark sits in silence for a minute or two waiting for Jonathan to return to his call, he begins thinking about his situation. Something inside him has come alive. He is definitely gravitating to Jonathan's ideas.

"I'm back, Father," Jonathan says. "It's already starting. That call I had to take, my boss wants me to come to your office right now and interview you. I didn't tell him I already had you on the phone. He said that there is a buzz about your appearance on the Jimmy Fallon Show last night, and you should expect several people from the media to be there at the church to interview you. Ocean Crest is about to go from a quiet beach town into a bit of media frenzy. I have to be there, so I'll drive down right away. I suggest you get ready for cameras and newspaper people to come to your office and camp out to get some interviews."

"Really?" Father Mark asks surprised. "How do you know this is going to happen?"

"We, in the media and news business, are all very well connected. Word spreads fast. With all the social media attention you're getting, this is very newsworthy. It is not every day that a Catholic priest tells the world that if Jesus came back to this Earth, he would be crucified again--and this time by the Catholics!"

"Okay, Jonathan, I get it. I need to get my head around this and decide what I'm going to say. The funny thing is that you may be the only one who shows up here!"

"I doubt it," retorts Jonathan. Father Mark can hear Jonathan moving around on the other end of the line. "I'm getting into my car and will head your way."

"Okay. See you soon, Jonathan."

Within ninety minutes news vans begin to pull up to St. Jude Church. They include the local networks, NJTV and New Jersey Network, as well as the major networks like ABC, CNN, and NBC. Also, writers from the *New York Times*, the *Wall Street Journal*, the *New York Post*, and the local New Jersey papers *The Record* and *The Wave,* are present. And, of course, so is Jonathan Crew from the *Star Ledger.*

As they gather, they ask Jonathan to go to the rectory door and ask for Father Mark and request that he come out and speak to the media. They all know about the article Jonathan wrote with Father Mark, and they know he has the best chance to convince him to come out and speak with them.

Monsignor Joseph, well aware of the goings on outside, stands by his office window that faces the street to see, one by one, the media vans and cars pulling up. He concludes this is getting very much out of hand. He walks to Father Mark's office and, before he gets through the office doorway, begins to say loudly, "Mark, do you see what's going on out here? There must be twenty or thirty people from the media on our front lawn. Cameras, microphones, everything! Then he says loudly and sternly, "This is exactly what I wanted to avoid. Exactly what I feared."

"Monsignor, I will take care of it. I will go out there and talk to them and have them leave."

"More talk," the Monsignor interrupts. "Just what we need, you talking more."

Father Mark decides to use his direct and firm communication capabilities. "Monsignor, I'm going to do the right thing here, but I'm suggesting you back off a bit. I know you're frustrated but let me take care of this."

"You better," the Monsignor responds with an irked tone, as he immediately turns around and walks out of Father Mark's office.

As the Monsignor leaves, Margaret enters to tell Father Mark that Jonathan Crew is at the front door asking for him to come out and address the media.

"Okay, Margaret." he utters in an exhausted tone, "I'll be right there." He gathers his thoughts and slowly walks out and down the stairs to the foyer. He stands at the closed front door for a few seconds then reaches for the door handle and steps outside.

By now, several of the local townspeople have gathered to see what the commotion is all about. As Father Mark reaches the top step, the media rushes to him and begins shouting a deluge of questions with microphones in hand and arms extended out. With so many questions being shouted out at him, he can hardly understand one from the next. However, one question breaks through the shouting: "Are you trying to disrupt the Catholic Church?"

Standing above them on the top of the cement landing above the five brick steps that lead to the sidewalk, Father Mark raises his hands high with palms facing the crowd, asking them to be quiet, and waits for the shouts to subside. They settle down, and he lowers his arms and begins to speak.

"Good morning. Please, everyone, give me a few minutes to say a few words and then I'm happy to answer some of your questions." He spots Jonathan Crew just behind the CNN reporter who has her arm extended out, microphone in hand. Jonathan gives Father Mark a supportive wink.

"It appears my participation on the Jimmy Fallon Show last night got quite a bit of attention. I'm well aware of the social media response and, yes, my email and phone have been barraged with messages. Let me first say that in no way am I trying to do any harm to the Catholic Church, and the great leaders of the Church, or the millions who are part of our great institution. I just have perspectives—somewhat unique perspectives. The Catholic Church is a great institution that does wonderful things for so many around the world. All I'm doing is sharing what I feel in my heart as I try to improve how we serve the world.

"I repeat, I'm a Catholic and being a priest serving this institution is an honor. I believe that many within our institution feel as I do, and I have heard them share some of the same views as I have. So, what is the message I've been delivering? It may not be totally understood, so let me clarify. What I have been communicating is CHANGE." Father Mark emphasizes the word *change*. "Change is good. We, as a Church, need to change. I understand that with change comes fear and uncertainty. It's always easier to stay as you are. But, with change, comes growth.

"Let me ask all of you a question. You don't need to answer me; just answer silently to yourselves. Do you have something in your life you want to change? Is there something you have known for a long time that needs to change but you just haven't committed to making the change? Or, candidly, are you fearful of the change? If you change what you're considering right now, will someone be upset? Will you alienate a friend or two? Will your husband or wife not like what you want to tell them about what you want to change? How about your job? Are you really happy? Have you been contemplating a change in your career?

"I'm asking these questions, because there is a high probability that many of you are thinking about some kind of change in your life. And maybe, like most people, you fear the unknown. You know deep down in your heart that the change will be good, but you're doubting yourself. That negative small voice pops up and questions you. What if you're wrong? What if the change makes you worse off? Here's the secret—ask God. Ask your inner spirit. Go to a quiet room in your home, close your eyes, and talk to God, whatever 'God' is to you. Talk to your inner spirit and ask questions. What answers come to mind? I know you'll get answers. If it isn't right then and there, they'll come when you least expect it."

The crowd of reporters and local neighbors listen attentively. Father Mark strikes a nerve in all of them. For these few minutes, this event transforms from reporters investigating Father Mark to Father Mark giving them valuable guidance.

"When you get those answers in the form of thoughts," Father Mark continues, "don't dismiss them. Those thoughts are coming from God, from your super conscious mind. Another way to program yourself to get the answers you need about a change you're considering is right before you go to bed. Tell yourself you will have dreams, and in those dreams will be guidance for the change you are thinking about. When you wake, write down the dreams you experienced. Think about them. Your super conscious mind will deliver ideas and answers through dreams. Again, if you don't get answers from your dreams, or you don't remember your dreams, don't be discouraged. Once again, thoughts will come to you when you least expect it, and those thoughts are triggered by your efforts of self-talk before you went to sleep.

"Now, back to the Church. We certainly have changed some, but I feel we can do much more. Just as I'm encouraging you to be brave and move forward with what *you* want to change, I would love to see the Church do the same. We need to take more responsibility for the abuses that priests have committed. We need to attract the youth of our society. We need to guide the young and old alike on how to live a better life one day at a time.

A single day of peace at a time. We must be careful to not let our traditions be an excuse for not reinventing ourselves. We must reinvent. My ideas, while all of them are not perfect, are meant to have us think deeply about our ways and face the brutal facts as to what is and what is not working.

"I appreciate that all of you are here today. Just as I suggest that we, as spiritual leaders, need to do more positive things, I hope your intention here today is to spread positive perspectives … and not to embellish my facts to sell more newspapers or TV ads, not just to have an interesting lead story on your upcoming news, or to find ways to condemn the Catholic Church.

"I'm sure you all have great things in your lives, and you all have challenges. Our job as spiritual leaders is to show you how to overcome your challenges and live a happy and successful life. That is why Jesus came here in the first place—to teach us, to change things for the better, to have us repent for our sins, and to teach us that there is life after death.

"I ask you all, how many of you would like to be happier and more at peace? I believe many, if not all of you, fall into that category. I'm speaking about topics that make us all think and re-evaluate ourselves. Some of these topics are difficult, but with addressing difficult topics and issues, we become stronger and better. I love the Catholic Church, and I'm grateful I can serve. Going forward, I will do my best to instigate positive change while being less controversial. Now, I'm happy to answer a few questions."

A woman reporter from NBC News shouts out as Father Mark stands confidently now, shoulders back, his hands folded in front of him. "Father, do you really think Catholics would crucify Jesus if he returned here on earth?"

Father Mark unfolds his hands, raises his right hand and gestures as he responds. "That statement I made last night seems to be the one that really got everyone going. As I said, I don't mean that we would put him up on a cross again, but the point I tried to make is, if he returned here and challenged what we're doing as a Church and suggested many changes, told us to take all the wealth we have and do something differently, would we object? Would we object to the point where we would discredit him? I don't know; it doesn't seem so far-fetched to me. I think Jesus would put an enormous amount of pressure on us to change, and I'm not so sure we would take kindly to his suggestions. Next question?"

The CNBC representative from the front row of reporters asks, "Have you heard from the Vatican regarding your views and all the attention you're getting?"

Father Mark chuckles, "You're giving me way too much credit. I doubt the Vatican has any awareness about me."

A female reporter from NJ.com questions, "Father, your views while somewhat controversial, seem to be resonating with many people. What is your plan to continue this and inspire more people?"

Father Mark then looks straight into the eyes of Jonathan Crew as he answers her. "I received that question just a little while ago from a good friend." Jonathan smiles, feeling pleased that Father Mark considers him a good friend. "I answered that I didn't know. I'm happy that I'm inspiring people, but I don't know how to continue other than what I do every day. I'm probably going to take some down time and think about things." Father Mark says this because of the notice he received that morning from Monsignor Joseph. He doesn't want the Monsignor to be in a difficult position of having put Father Mark on suspension. "I'll think about it. That's the best answer I can give right now."

"Father Mark," screams out a writer from the *Wall Street Journal*, "What are the local Catholic leaders feeling and saying about your views and recent fame?"

Father Mark pauses at this, and he knows he has to be deliberate with this answer. Above, at the second-floor casement window, with it cranked open a few inches so he can hear the conversations below, Monsignor Joseph stands quietly listening to the dialog. This question gets his attention even more. He leans closer to the window to be sure he hears Father Mark's response. "We have a great support system within the entire Catholic Church. The same goes for our diocese. We support various views while we try to stay true to our mission." Monsignor Joseph is relieved with the answer.

The *Wall Street Journal* reporter follows up his question with, "So, they agree with your views one hundred percent?"

"I wouldn't say one hundred percent," Father Mark responds rapidly.

Monsignor Joseph leans out further, almost bumping his head on the window, trying not to miss a word of this response. "None of us agree with everything from each other. That is what makes the world a special place—so many people and views. We just need to get better at respecting each other's views and consider them."

Father Mark realizes that he has, thus far, handled this communication very well, and he wants to put this media interview to an end. "So, let me thank you all for coming out here today. I need to go back to my meetings and ministering. I would greatly appreciate it if you all left this beautiful beach town as you found it and let us get back to our sleepy state of affairs.

"Go and serve one another and love one another. And, of course, think about what I shared with you about change. You have the power to change the things you want to change. With God, all things are possible." With that, Father Mark gives them a peace sign with his right hand raised. As he turns around to walk back into the rectory, the crowd of reporters shout more questions. Father Mark continues to walk back into the rectory waving his right hand just above his head with his fingers giving the peace sign. He then disappears behind the closing door.

CHAPTER 15

For the next few hours, Father Mark rests in his bedroom thinking deeply about what had transpired over the last month. Later he goes downstairs to get some food in the kitchen and, as he walks by Margaret, he sees a stack of message notes about two inches thick. Margaret looks very fatigued. "Margaret, what's this stack of messages?"

She looks up at Father Mark. "They're all the phone calls you received today. I don't know what to do. The phone won't stop ringing and just about every call is for you." Before she can continue, the phone rings again. She looks at Father Mark with an expression that says, *Here we go again.*

Margaret greets the caller. "Thank you for calling St. Jude Church. How can I help you? No, I'm sorry. Father Mark is not here and won't be returning for some time. He's taking some time off." She pauses as she listens to the caller. "Sure, I'll take a message but, like I said, he's away for some time, so you probably won't get a return call for a long while, if at all." With that, Margaret begins writing quickly on the message pad and then says, "Okay, I have it. Thank you for calling," and she hangs up the phone. "Yep, another one for you, Father."

"I'm so sorry. I don't know how long this is going to go on, but I can't have you deal with this all day long. Let's do this: let's route all the calls to a greeting that I set up, and we won't take messages. I'll explain to all the callers that I'm on sabbatical and won't be able to return the calls."

"That would be great, Father. Thank you." Margaret is relieved.

"I know how to do this. I'll take care of it right now." With that, he walked into his office picked up the phone, clicked the voice mail code, entered his password, and then pressed a number on the handset to allow him to leave a message on the voice mail. "This is Father Mark, and I thank you for your call. I thank you and the many others who have called to share your views on my recent communications. I have decided to take a bit of a sabbatical, so I won't be able to respond to your call. As this is the case, I cannot accept messages, but if it is an emergency and you need spiritual guidance, please call Monsignor Joseph here in the rectory. But please, don't call him if it's me you want to talk to. Again, thank you for your interest in speaking to me, and I wish you God's blessings." Father Mark pressed the pound sign on the handset and then hung up.

Father Mark had lost his appetite. He got up from his chair and went to see Margaret again. "Okay, Margaret, that should do it. You may get some calls on the Monsignor's line, but I asked people not to call him and try to reach me that way. We'll see." Then he reaches out and picks up the stack of phone messages and takes them to his office. He sits on the couch under the window and begins to read. *Amazing*, he thinks. *I can't believe all these people called. Most of them I don't even know.*

Then he takes his iPhone out of his front pants pocket and, as he has it on silent mode since last night, it lights up without a tone showing a text is received. It keeps lighting up as one text after another arrives. He places it on his desk, closes his eyes for a few seconds, and then slowly shakes his head not believing so many messages are coming to him. He opens his eyes and has a sudden desire for a cup of coffee. As he goes to the kitchen to prepare his java, he sees a text come from Jonathan Crew. It reads, "Do you have a minute for a phone call?"

Hmm, he thinks with a bit of sarcasm. *I wonder what Jonathan would like to talk about.* Without responding, he clicks on Jonathan's number to initiate a call.

"Father Mark, I'm so glad you called." Jonathan sounds pleased to hear back from him. "You had some crowd in front of the rectory. I'm sorry we interrupted your day, and I'm sorry that I came to your door to see if you would come and speak to us. It's just that they all know about the article I wrote about you, and they knew we had developed a friendship."

"It's okay, Jonathan. What can I do for you now?"

"Father, I hope I didn't cross the line, but I took the liberty to call a friend of mine who is one of the executives for 60 Minutes. It's just that I know your voice needs to be heard, and every time you speak you inspire people. Like today, you came out to talk to the reporters and somehow you shifted the focus of aggressive media people who are looking for a great story to a point where you had us all thinking about what changes we should make in our lives. That doesn't happen with the media. I can tell you. We're like tigers, and you're the meat. The media can eat people alive, but not you."

"Hold on, Jonathan," interrupted Father Mark, "when are you going to get to the part as to why you called 60 Minutes?"

"O-okay," stutters Jonathan. "Being curious if they had been aware of your Jimmy Fallon appearance, I wanted to know if they would like to have you on 60 Minutes." And, without giving Father Mark a chance to respond, Jonathan continues quickly, "I told them that you knew nothing about me calling them, and if they had any interest, they would have to deal directly with you. I told them that I have been so inspired by you that I believe that the more people who hear your perspectives, the better the world will be. And, it will make a great 60 Minutes story."

Father Mark is intrigued and asks, "How did they respond?"

"My friend is very interested. He knew of my story about you, he watched the Jimmy Fallon show, and he said he thought you are an excellent guest with an intriguing message. He, too, felt inspired by what you spoke about. He needed to talk with a few other executives to see if they agreed. He called me ten minutes later and said they want to do a segment on you within the next two weeks! Again, Father Mark, I'm sorry, I want to be respectful of you and don't want to do anything to upset you, but you are special. You have a great message."

Father Mark responds, "Text me the name and number of the person I need to call at 60 Minutes, and I will decide. I know you mean well Jonathan, but I want your word that you will not do this again. You will not call any network, news media, no one, without talking to me first."

"You have my word, Father. I won't," responded Jonathan in an apologizing tone. "What are you going to do during your sabbatical?"

"You know, Jonathan, I just need to step back and re-evaluate things. I think the Church can use a break from me, and I will take some down time."

Jonathan is a bit confused. "What will you do with yourself? You thrive by helping others. You're committed to giving people one day of peace."

"Yes, you're correct, Jonathan. I'll figure that out. Whatever I do and wherever I go, I'll find a way to spread peace."

"Okay, Father, but please keep me posted on what you decide to do."

"You have my word. Send me the text. We'll talk soon."

Father Mark let two days go by as he considered what he would do with his life while on sabbatical. During those two days, he read as many texts, emails, and social media posts that he could. The last two nights he stayed up past 2 a.m. reading all the responses. A part of him really enjoys the limelight. It reminds him of how he felt during his days in the technology world running businesses and that feeling of people valuing his insights.

But, more than the attention, he enjoys the feeling that he positively connects with thousands of people. While he received his share of hate mail via text, email, and social media, he feels satisfied by the number of people who agree with his perspectives. It's further confirmation that his view of spirituality resonates with people. So many people share their support, and that inspires him. He knows he is making a positive difference.

Three days after Jonathan's text sharing the contact for the executive at 60 Minutes, Father Mark feels a bit exhausted but at peace. He picks up his phone and finds the text Jonathan sent him. Something tells him he shouldn't pass up this opportunity to spread spirituality to a national and maybe even a global audience. He looks at the name and phone number pauses a moment. Then, he says aloud to himself, "Here goes nothing," and dials the number.

The call between Father Mark and the 60 Minutes executive, Nancy Torres, lasts about twenty minutes. He explains his interest in being a guest on 60 Minutes but wants to first understand the details. Nancy Torres is very thorough and outlines everything in order to make him feel comfortable. She discusses when they would shoot the segment, where it would take place, how 60 Minutes will determine which anchor personality will lead the story, and how long it will take.

One of the contingencies Nancy tells him is that they have to record this segment over the next five days, because they would need to get it on the air within two weeks. Father Mark's story is very popular right now and letting too much time go by would make it less relevant. Father Mark asks for twenty-four hours to make up his mind and Nancy agrees, but she tells him that she can't assure him 60 Minutes will continue to have interest if he delays much further.

CHAPTER 16

At 8 a.m. the next morning, Father Mark being up for three hours already, goes for a brief run along the beach and then sits at the water's edge on the sand to pray and think. He returns to the rectory, showers, and feels ready for the day ahead. He picks up his iPhone and calls Nancy Torres at 60 Minutes.

"Good morning, this is Nancy," a friendly voice greets him.

"Nancy, this is Father Mark Tossi. And good morning to you, too."

"It's great to hear from you, Father. Have you made up your mind?" Nancy asks, getting right to the point.

"I have. I'm going to do this, and I hope I don't regret it!"

"That's fantastic!" Nancy says enthusiastically. "You won't regret this at all. Let's put a plan together to get this done."

Nancy and Father Mark discuss the logistics and agree that in two days Father Mark will visit the CBS studios in New York City at 10 a.m. sharp. That will be a Wednesday and gives the CBS crew enough time to record and edit the segment to get it on the air for Sunday evening's show. She can't commit to who will do the interview as that will have to be decided by the executive producer.

After hanging up the phone, he experiences both excitement and nervousness. His prime-time TV debut during which over ten million people will be watching is only days away. He thinks to himself that he should begin preparing what he will talk about. Then, he suddenly stops himself. Speaking out loud he says, "I'm not going to prepare anything. I'm going to go in and do this interview and let God speak through me. If I prepare too much, I will be too calculated, not spontaneous enough, and I may block out the spirit of God trying to speak through me." Just then he feels a great sense of calm. He smiles and, in this peaceful feeling, feels confident that this is the right way to proceed.

During the next two days, Father Mark begins preparing what course his life will take after the 60 Minutes interview. Over the last few days, something Jonathan Crew had said to him continues to play over and over in his mind. Jonathan convinced Father Mark that he offers great teachings for society. If Jonathan is correct, then Father Mark feels he should deliver those messages. He has an idea as to how he can do that. After many of hours of phone calls, sending emails, and communicating over the Internet, he has it all arranged. Again, he feels the peace of knowing his plan is in place. Then he calls Jonathan Crew.

"Hello Father, so happy to receive your call," Jonathan greets him.

"Thank you, Jonathan. Do you mind if I get right to the point? I'm pretty busy and I need your help."

"Sure Father. Anything. What can I do for you?"

Father Mark takes a deep breath. "I have a couple of things to share with you. First, I'm going to do the 60 Minutes show. I get interviewed this week, and it will air Sunday night."

Jonathan is excited for Father Mark. "That's great news, Father."

"Easy for you to say, Jonathan, but I want you to know that I'm very thankful for you and for making this possible. After the show, I'm going to take a trip. I will be out of the country for about a month. Maybe longer. While I'm gone, from time to time, I'm going to email you some things that I will need you to organize. Will you do that for me?"

A bit confused, Jonathan responds, "Sure, but where will you be going, and what will you be sending me?"

"You'll know that in due time but, right now, I just need to know you'll organize what I send you. You have told me several times that I have a great message to share, and we're going to see if you're right."

Jonathan, still confused, says, "Well … okay. Whatever you need, Father. But how will I know how to organize what you're sending me when I don't yet know what it is you will be sending?"

"It will come together easily for you. I promise. Thank you for helping me. You have become a very good friend. Now, I have to run, but I'll be in touch one way or the other."

"One way or the other?" Jonathan questions, not knowing what Father Mark is referring to.

He concludes the call and says, "Be well, Jonathan. We'll talk soon." He hangs up before Jonathan has a chance to respond.

Jonathan realizes the call ends and looks at it with a very confused expression. He can't comprehend Father Mark's intentions.

Father Mark arrives Wednesday morning in New York City early enough so he can go to Saint Patrick's Cathedral to sit, think, and pray inside the magnificent structure. Being a beautiful warm morning, before going into the church, he walks several blocks between 5th Avenue and 50th Street where the historic church is located. He walks north as far at 60th street and then turns right. Then he walks one block to Madison Avenue, makes a right on Madison and returns to 50th street. His pace is soft and casual. It's an enjoyable walk, and he exudes positive energy from seeing many people hustling around the city. Again, memories of his business days flood in. While completely at peace with his decision to pursue the priesthood, he does miss the action of the business world. Entering Saint Patrick's, Father Mark finds himself to be very relaxed.

He sits at the far-left end of a pew about midway on the right side of the church. He looks around, taking in all the beauty of this magnificent structure. Being there many times through the years never diminishes the joy of returning. The architecture is so beautiful to him. Praying relaxes him. He prays for guidance. He knows this upcoming interview with 60 Minutes will be a defining experience, and he wants to communicate well. Most importantly, he wants to be sure he delivers the right messages.

He folds his hands on his lap, slowly closes his eyes, takes a few very deep breaths to help him get into a spiritual state, and prays for guidance. Then, he just allows his mind to go blank—to not concentrate on any created thoughts. The objective is to allow spiritual thoughts to enter his mind. A thunderous voice does not appear, no clear-cut message, and no revelation. But, after approximately twenty minutes of this quiet silence, he feels extremely relaxed. He opens his eyes, and a warm calm flow throughout his body. He is ready.

He arrives at the CBS studios on West 57th Street promptly at 10 a.m. He is intentionally dressed in black paints, a black shirt, and white clerical collar traditional for most Catholic priests. He wants to be viewed as a Catholic. He wants it to be clear to the 60 Minutes audience that he is not transitioning away from the Catholic Church.

He is greeted by Kyle Ambrose, who is the executive producer for 60 Minutes. Kyle exudes friendliness but with a very business-like demeanor. Ambrose had welcomed hundreds of guests during his seventeen years at 60 Minutes. They included U.S. presidents, executives, politicians, entrepreneurs, athletes, Wall Street leaders, philanthropists, world leaders, you name it.

Kyle expertly briefs Father Mark and, for the first time, Father Mark learns who would be conducting the interview. "We decided that Scott Pelley would be the right person to interview you, Father. His laid-back style is one we feel matches your personality. However, he will ask you some difficult questions. Here's a list of some of those questions, but I want you to know that he will ad-lib a bit. He may hear you say something or just get a gut feeling that he should go in a completely different direction ... and he will. So, no guarantees that he will follow this line of questioning." While explaining, Kyle reaches out to hand Father Mark the list of questions.

"Thank you, but I'd rather not see the questions in advance. I, too, would rather go with the flow and not prepare. I think it will be more genuine."

While that wasn't the first time Kyle Ambrose had gotten that reaction from a guest, it certainly was one of very few. Most people being interviewed for a national and global audience wanted some idea of what questions they would get. "That's brave," Kyle responds as he takes the paper back.

Father Mark gives Kyle a confident wink. "We're good."

Next up is the makeup room where some subtle refinements are made to even out his complexion and reduce any shine the bright camera lights might create. After fifteen minutes with a makeup expert, Father Mark enters the backstage cafe, where he requests only a bottle of water.

As he walks into the studio, he observes how well it mimics a formal living room. "Wow! Very impressive. You guys know how to make this look like a real living room. No one would ever know this is really recorded in a New York City studio."

"I'll take that as a compliment, Father," commented Molly Wallace, the set manager, as she walks toward him. "I've created some very interesting sets in my day." Molly is a youthful looking woman in her mid-forties who has complete control of all the goings on.

"Okay," Molly instructs, "Father Mark is going to sit here on this chair." Molly points to a dark, formal wooden chair with a red velvet seat cushion and high back. "Scott will sit here on Father Mark's left." Molly points to an identical chair but with a blue velvet seat cushion. I want filled water glasses on this table between them. Now, Father, please sit here so I can do a brief test. Turn on the show lights, please," Molly shouts.

With that command, the set explodes with bright lights, and Father Mark feels a bit intimidated as he momentarily becomes blinded by the sudden burst of light. "Let me get behind the camera and see how he looks." Molly moves briskly behind camera #1. "Okay, looks good," she confirms. "Now let me see from the others."

When she gets to camera #4, she stops. "We need more makeup on his left forehead. It's shining from camera #4." Todd, a makeup expert, rushes over and places a bit of tan makeup on Father Mark's forehead and spreads it around to even it out. "Step aside, Todd, and let me see now." Todd steps away so the camera has a full shot on Father Mark. "Perfect. Nice work Todd. Thank you."

Father Mark begins to feel a little nervous with all the lights, makeup, and cameras rolling around to different angles. He takes a few deep breaths to get oxygen into his lungs and to calm the nervous feeling.

"Okay, we're almost ready to start," Molly announces. She then goes over to Father Mark and puts out her right hand to shake his. "Father, you're going to do great. I'm really looking forward to this interview. I saw you on Jimmy Fallon, and I loved it. Thank you for doing this."

Father Mark shakes her hand. "Thank you. I hope I do as well as you think I will."

Then Molly shares, "I'm out. Rick, the director, takes it from here."

Rick Mansone comes over to Father Mark and, after introducing himself, begins explaining what will take place. He wears a headset with a microphone attached and has the ability to communicate with anyone throughout the studio. A wire runs from the headset to inside his shirt and out to a square power unit attached to his belt on the left side of his waist. "So, here is how this all works, Father. It's really pretty simple. The entire interview will be done here. We're not going on location anywhere, so this is going to be very easy. All you need to do is put your mind in the state that you're having a conversation with Scott Pelley, and that's it. Try not to look into any of the cameras, because we want the feeling of a conversation. Scott asks you questions, and you give answers. Simple. If you ever need a break, when Scott is asking his next question or making a clarifying statement, you just raise your right hand, and we cut the filming. This isn't live, so there's no pressure. We can take as long as you'd like. Scott is the inquisitive type, so he is really good at asking provocative questions and digging deep. You just take your time and answer as you would like to. Easy ... right?"

"Sure, sounds that way," Father Mark replies.

Then Rick presses a button on the power unit attached to his belt and says, "We're ready for Scott down here. Ready to get started." Father Mark takes a few sips of water from the glass on the table between his chair and where Scott will be sitting. He knows it is show time.

Scott Pelley enters the room from the opposite side of the set and stagehands greet him to touch up his makeup and straighten out his jacket and tie to get him exactly as they need him to look on camera. Scott exudes professionalism, wearing a solid blue two-piece suit with a white dress shirt and red tie with a faint pattern of thin blue lines running through it.

Then Scott walks over to Father Mark. "Hello, Father Mark," he greets him warmly as they shake hands. "I'm so looking forward to this interview. I have read as much as I can about you, and I must have watched the Jimmy Fallon interview six or seven times—all in the interests of preparation. I also researched other spiritual leaders who share some of your philosophies. I hope you realize you have become a sort of celebrity. Your Christian and spiritual views are somewhat unique, and many people are feeling connected to them. Any questions before we get started?"

"No, I'm good."

With that, Scott and Father Mark take their respective seats. Rick Mansone stands in front of them both and shouts out, "The Father Mark interview ... Take 1. He then walks away from the sightline of the cameras and the interview begins.

"Father Mark, it is a pleasure to have you with us," Scott Pelley states.

"Thank you," Father Mark responds and, before Scott can ask a question, Father Mark queries, "So, Mr. Pelley, why is it that 60 Minutes finds me so interesting that you would like to do an interview with me?"

Scott smiles. "Well, it appears you have basically shaken up the Catholic Church by expressing views not often, if ever, expressed by a Catholic priest—views on abortion, Jesus being crucified again, how the Church has not been held accountable for the abuses they have done, and how the Catholic Church is not changing with the times and can become obsolete. And, what is interesting is that millions of people are responding positively to your messages.

"Now, did you know," and Scott looks down at the notes he has prepared, "that over the last thirty days between Facebook, Twitter, Instagram, LinkedIn, and YouTube, you've been mentioned over one million times? This is the kind of activity celebrities like Oprah Winfrey get. You have become a social media sensation. Athletes, actors and actresses, political leaders, spiritual leaders, business leaders, and hundreds of thousands of others are commenting about you. Why do you think that is?"

Father Mark smiles and responds calmly and confidently. "I feel this confirms that what I'm saying is what many have been thinking for quite a while. I feel I have been the voice of what people are feeling."

Scott quickly asks, "I don't ever recall hearing anyone state the case that if Jesus Christ returned here that he would be crucified again, potentially by the Catholics. Have you?"

Father Mark smiles again and nods. "That comment seems to have gotten the most attention. To answer your question, Scott, no, I don't ever recall hearing that from a leader in the Catholic Church, or anyone for that matter."

Scott Pelley nods his head quickly confirming his agreement.

"Here is why I made that statement, and I have said this before. We, the Catholic Church may not have it right. Yes, we are very charitable and we do amazing positive things around the world. But, let's face it, we've made some very big mistakes. We have so much wealth, so many rules, and I don't think we've evolved as well as we should have, especially over the last thirty to forty years. The world has changed. To remain great and have a positive impact on people, we have to change appropriately.

"My point is that if Jesus did return and he saw what we're doing, would he congratulate us and tell us we have it perfect? I don't think so. By the way, this goes for all formal religions. I believe he would make some very strong suggestions that could change the very fabric of our institution.

"I believe he would ask us to change, just as he told the people and chief priests the first time he walked the earth. We all have to evolve and change. Families do, corporations do, relationships do, and friendships do. To stay relevant and to be strong, we have to adjust."

Scott interjects, "Are you saying the Catholic Church doesn't make changes?"

"No, I'm not saying that. I'm saying we're not making enough changes. We're living on ritual. Just look at how difficult it is to get the younger generation to come to church. Can't we do something different to make the church experience more inspiring, so we impact more people?"

Scott navigates to the next question. "I read a story about your Easter homily and how you told your congregation that they shouldn't donate money to the Church and, instead, they should find a cause they're passionate about and give the money there. Why did you recommend that?"

Father Mark leans forward in his chair, pleased this question is being posed. "My perspective is that we, the leaders of the Catholic Church, tend to make people feel they need to do this or do that to be a great Catholic, in order to enter the Kingdom of Heaven. Here's my point: Do you think God cares if you decide not to give money to the church but instead give money elsewhere to a great cause? I don't think He or She does. What God cares about is that we do good here on Earth.

"I don't think God cares if you're Catholic, Jewish, Protestant, etc. What She or He cares about is that we fulfill our potential, love one another, have gratitude, love and respect God, execute spiritual leadership, make this world a better place for everyone … those kinds of things are what matters. The formal religions, in my opinion, try to create these rules that we should follow so that we are part of their religious organization."

"Father, you refer to God as He or She. What is God? Is God a man or a woman?"

Father Mark smiles and sits back in his chair looking very confident. "We humans try to humanize God. We try to see God in the way our minds work. So, we say 'He' most of the time. I believe God is neither. No one knows what God is, but I believe God is an energy, a light, and a power. God created the endless Universe. God is the Universe. God's power is infinite. God put His or Her energy and power into each of us. We are all god-like. And, if we tap into it and have faith, we can do amazing things. Didn't Jesus teach the people this when he said, "You can do even greater things than these?" So, in my mind and soul, I see God as the almighty power and an energy source."

"Father, is it a sin to be gay?"

"Not in my eyes," responds Father Mark. "I know the formal religions try to make the gay community feel they are sinning, that they will not enter the Kingdom of Heaven because of their sexual preference. I just don't believe that. Let's face it, being gay isn't easy. So many men and woman who are gay say if they had a choice and would change their inner feelings, they would be straight. They have endured so much struggle being gay.

"We should all know by now that being gay isn't just a choice. There's something in your DNA that has you preferring the same sex. So, what are they to do, ignore it and fake a fulfilled relationship with someone of the opposite sex, else they are sinning? This is too complex of a situation to just label it as a sin. In my view, the all-forgiving God, the all-loving God, isn't going to reject a man or a woman because they are gay. God understands. And I know the Bible says a man shall leave his mother and father and take a woman as his wife. I don't know ... it sounds so perfect, and it is for so many, but what about the rights of people who aren't made that way. They are great people, too. God isn't judging."

Scott again alters the course of the conversation. "So, if you could say one thing to the world to help them be happier, what would it be?"

Father Mark pauses, shifts his eyes up and to the right as he thinks about the question. "If I suggested just one thing to help people become happier, it would be what Jesus taught us. Love your neighbor as thyself. It is through giving love that you get love. Give love and you feel amazingly happy. It's hard to do, but if you do it, you'll get fantastic results.

"Loving your neighbor is, of course, loving everyone—mostly to those who did you harm in some way. When I say 'love them' I'm suggesting you send them loving and positive vibes. It comes back to you in spades. How about you, Scott, can you think of someone in your business life or personal life who did you harm and deep down you still have ill feelings for him or her?"

Scott shifts slightly in his seat and seems a bit nervous. He touches the right side of his nose with his index finger, which some body language experts will tell you is a sign that the person may not be comfortable with what they're hearing. "I suppose I do, Father. Sure, I do. So, how do I just totally and completely love that person?"

"I'm glad you asked, because I suspect most of your viewers are asking the same question. Someone has hurt them at some time in their life, and they still hold resentment. Step one is just tell God you forgive them. Forgiveness does not require you to be totally good with the harm that you experienced. You can still feel angry, but the forgiveness process is telling God you are now okay with it.

"So, after you forgive, hope for good things for that person. Sending positive vibes to them is the love. If you do this over and over and send love and positive vibes to all who are around you, you will feel an amazing sense of happiness and power. Try it Scott. Scott, will you try it right now?"

Feeling awkward, Scott asks, "You mean you're asking me to publicly forgive this person here on the air?"

"Scott, I suggest you leave the name out, out of respect for you and that person. The world doesn't have to know who the person is."

Scott Pelley takes a deep breath and shifts in his seat again. "Okay, Father, I'll give this a try." He then pauses for a few seconds in silence.

The entire studio staff freezes waiting for Scott's response. No one moves throughout the studio. Father Mark has a soft smile on his face, knowing Scott is going to do something very special.

"Okay, Father." Scott says, "God, I'm thinking of someone who did me wrong. You know whom I'm thinking of. I want to forgive that person right now. So, I do forgive ... I forgive this person, and I ask that you do, too." Scott then closes his eyes as if in brief prayer or meditation and says softly, "I send love and great things to this person. I hope this person recognizes their error in behavior and asks for forgiveness. I'm sending great things to this person ... and love."

Scott opens his eyes, and Father Mark smiles at him without uttering a word. He waits for Scott to proceed. "Wow! That did feel good!" Scott relaxes and leans back in his chair seemingly relieved.

"Of course, it felt good, Scott. You just did a god-like thing, and you are blessed for it." Then Father Mark does what the executive director instructed him not to do. He looks straight into camera #3 and says, "I ask all of you who are watching tonight to do the same exact thing. Do it tonight, before you go to bed. I promise you will feel what Scott just felt," and he adds with enthusiasm, "and you will have a great night's sleep! Doing this will give you a great sense of peace, and the person you are forgiving will feel that peace. They will not know where it's coming from, but they will feel the forgiveness. If you all do this tonight, millions of people will have a single day of peace. How beautiful is that?"

A few seconds of silence pass, and then Scott continues. "That felt very good, Father, thank you. Let me shift gears a bit. Today's political landscape is pretty ugly. Maybe never before have the different sides of the isle been in so much disagreement with the other. One of the things that has gotten out of hand is what appears to be the hatred between the parties. How do we fix this and get the two sides of the political landscape more aligned with one another? Can spiritual leaders help bridge the gap between the people?"

Father Mark adjusts himself in his chair to get more comfortable. "The political fighting is a difficult one to solve. That said, I do feel that our political leaders need to be less about …," Father Mark then points his right index finger at Scott Pelley and shifts his finger to point at himself and keeps repeating this movement from Scott to himself several times as he says, "who is right and more about …," Father Mark then opens his arms wide as if to welcome someone with a hug, "…what is right." If we move away from *who* is right and more to *what* is right, good things happen. If they do this, I suspect there would be more cooperation. Sorry, no easy answers here. But it begins with less ego and more giving to others.

"Then it comes down to you, the news media. You turn on CNN and you hear one side, turn on FOX and you hear the other. Personal agendas and political desires are what these news outlets are promoting. This isn't news--they have an agenda. They should start every show with a statement something like, 'Everything about our show is to promote our personal agenda and political desires. All our guests have been selected to persuade you to our beliefs.' They should have that stream along the bottom of the screen during the entire show. Respectfully, Scott, the media is a big part of creating the hatred that is going on.

"Unfortunately, the media is infecting the youth with their selfish views. I want us all to do a better job of inspiring our youth. If our population of youngsters can be taught that God loves them and gives them the power to do just about anything they set their hearts on, they'll grow to be optimistic people. They need to be taught the power of thought … that the thoughts they think about the most are the ones that come true. This is one of the most valuable secrets people need to uncover. We become the thoughts we think. God gave us that power.

"If you visualize yourself as if you already are the person you want to become, you bring God's and the Universe's energy to you to create that. We need to teach this to our children. Parents and teachers need to teach this. You can change your life at any age if you follow this secret and change your thoughts. You are never too young or too old to make a change in your life by changing the thoughts you think. There are so many good books that cover this topic. I recommend everyone watching to go buy and read any of those books and apply this principle.

"I know I'm getting off your question about politics, but this is really important. Let me present my case about the power of thoughts and how we all have to make a conscious effort to cancel out negative thoughts and replace them with positive thoughts.

"Scott, have you ever met or interacted with someone who has a negative slant on most things they're involved with? They criticize people, they're opinionated, and their tone is not uplifting but more derogatory. These are the same people who often find themselves on the short end of things, and then they become even more negative and point out how things never go right for them.

"This entire process snowballs and the negative gets stronger and stronger. What they need to do is consciously change their tone and attitude to be more grateful and positive. They need to see the positive side of things more, and then they'll start to experience more and more good things in their lives.

"Now, we all have negative thought moments. I certainly do, but those of us who catch ourselves being negative and consciously stop ourselves and replace those thoughts with productive, positive thoughts and statements attract more positive things in our lives. This said, we all must understand that even if we are the most positive people in the world, we will still have challenges in our lives. Things will go wrong, sometimes very wrong, such as illness, death, breakups, loss of a job, etc. BUT, if we keep our faith in God and believe that God has a great plan for us, we'll get over these miserable times more quickly and get back on track to better and more peaceful things going on in our lives."

Scott Pelley leans forward indicating his interest in this topic on positive thinking. "You know, Father, this is something most people have a hard time with. It's very interesting what you're talking about here. I'm not sure most people buy into the idea that they can create their own destiny—that by simply repeating positive statements to themselves and visualizing themselves as the person they want to become makes that happen. How do we encourage them to believe in this?"

Father Mark's grin shows his pleasure with the question, "First off, in the Bible, Jesus stated several times and in various ways that we have this power. For example, Jesus said, 'Whatsoever ye desire, when ye pray, believe that ye receive it and ye shall have it.' So, in essence, he instructs us to visualize that we already have what we're praying for … to use the power of belief and the power of faith and we will attract to us the things we want.

"But here is my suggestion to everyone out there…." Once again, Father Mark looks directly into camera #3 and says with passion in his voice, "I would like every single one of you out there to do a few things. If you do these things, I promise you will see results. First, write down two or three things you want in your life. Write them down in a way that starts with *Every moment in every day, I'm attracting into my life* …. and you put down what you want. Maybe it's a new job, a new relationship, a better financial situation, to be free of sickness, a calm state of mind, or whatever it is.

"Now, I'm asking you to read these things out loud at least three times a day and, as you're saying them, see yourself having the new job, being totally healthy, having the new relationship, being more mentally calm, or whatever. Do this for a month and you will see things changing. Keep doing it after one month and add more things you want and need. But, keep in mind, God will work on the timing that is right for you. We all want what we want NOW, but God knows when it's right for you. You need to be patient.

"The second thing I would like you to do is every time you feel or think or say something negative, cancel it by saying something like *cancel that thought* and replace it with a positive thought, feeling, or statement. Do this every day and night. I know for certain that, if you do this, you will soon start to feel better inside. You will have an attitude that uplifts your spirit and, almost magically, people and events will come your way to add positive things to your life."

Then Father Mark turns away from camera #3 and looks at Scott again. "So, to answer your question as to how can we encourage people to do what I'm suggesting, if they try doing what I just explained, they'll see things differently and feel differently. Positive things will come to their lives. They will have a single day of peace over and over. All they have to do is try it, and peace and happiness will be theirs."

"You certainly are convincing, Father. I have to give you that!" Scott displays a huge smile. "Here's my next question but, first, let me frame it. There continues to be some animosity towards big business. People feel that some dominant companies do not treat their people as well as they should. The CEO and other executives make significantly more than most of the people they employ. Here is my question: Is there a place for spirituality in corporate leadership? Through spirituality, can we connect better with our employees and have a more successful company?"

"I believe the answer is yes, one hundred percent. I call it spiritual leadership. Here's how I see it. First, you and some of your viewers may know that before I became a priest, I held a position as an executive in the technology industry. For the sake of time, I won't go into the details right now, but I had a very negative and traumatic thing take place in my life that I had to deal with. At first, I dealt with it very poorly and became a fraction of my old self. I basically became destitute. My mind, emotions, and spirit were in such a bad, dark place and, hence, I attracted negative things to me.

"So, the things I'm suggesting to people I have already done, and I turned my life around. Here's how I think spirituality has a place in business leadership." Father Mark once again leans forward in his chair, his eyes focused more deeply on Scott. "I see spirituality as doing things right and doing right by people all within the understanding that business is BUSINESS and the game is to win. Win ethically and morally but ... WIN. So, if I'm a leader and I first and foremost care about my team, they feel it. That creates trust. Now you have to do things to show them you care, like helping them set goals, holding them accountable for their performance, coaching them so they perform their best, showing them how they can advance their career for their personal benefit, give transparent feedback and, equally important, have fun with them.

"When employees are not performing well, you should have the difficult conversations with them in a professional way. As I said, the objective of business is to achieve the goals you set ... to win. So, I'm not recommending an environment of softness and passiveness. If you lead with strength blended with spirituality and a positive attitude, your people feel it. They feel your spiritual leadership, and they become more connected to you. Even if you have to fire someone, they feel you are doing it in a way that is honorable. They know you gave them all you had and, for some reason, this job just didn't work out. There may be some ill feelings, but those feelings will pass, because the terminated employee will know you did the right thing for all involved.

"Spiritual leadership is very different from leadership that just cares about the employees' performances for the sake of executive bonuses or company success. In my opinion, too many leaders think they care about their teams but, when you investigate further and ask deeper questions about their motivations, you find that the only motivation is their personal and corporate success. You see this in sports with coaches, in education with teachers and college professors, and you even see it in religions and their leaders.

"People know when you really care, they accept tough love, and they are very loyal. And then, they perform their best, so everyone wins. Spiritual leadership is the way to create a culture that drives organizational performance. Spiritual leadership creates a culture where everyone wins and compensation is more evenly shared."

"So, Father, have any leaders of companies reached out to you to have you help them become better leaders?"

"Yes, some have, and it's interesting how this began. Several business leaders came to me privately for counseling in various personal areas—family challenges, situations with children, relationship dilemmas. Then what happens is that we get into the business conversation and how well they connect with their team, and I share with them the components in what I call the spiritual leadership wheel … the components of being a spiritual leader.

"They eventually have the divine light bulb go off in their heads, and they see how spiritual leadership can help them with their career, family, children, and relationships. Some business leaders then ask me to participate in their company meetings to help everyone on their team execute spiritual leadership. I love doing those events, because you see how you help so many people change and become great leaders."

"So, Father," Scott shifts direction, "I would categorize you as a liberal priest. Many of your views are not what the Catholic Church subscribes to. I would also say that many spiritual leaders don't subscribe to your ideas. You are more of a spiritual leader who encourages people to use their talents, their power—or, as you say, the power God gave them—to go help others and not just sit inside and pray and think about God, but to go out and do something to make themselves and the world a better place. And, all the while, they should feel good about themselves, even if they're not following the Catholic religion by the book."

"I couldn't have said it any better, Scott." Father Mark opens his arms and hands to welcome the point Scott makes.

In a pointed way, Scott pursues this topic. "Then, what do you think about monks who are in seclusion or cloistered nuns who are cut off from society as they pray in isolation, believing this behavior will help humanity, relieve suffering, and that their sacrifice will lead to the salvation of the world?"

"I'm not here to judge." Father Mark runs his fingers through his dark black hair. "People who dedicate their entire lives to prayer in isolation have chosen a great sacrifice. I don't know what God thinks about this, but I do feel that if these people got out and used their immense spirituality to connect with others, to help and counsel people while they prayed deeply, there may be more good done in this way. That said, they believe that by their personal sacrifice, God puts more mercy on everyone else and this world is less painful because of what they do. We should all be thankful for what they're doing. God is speaking to them too, and that is why they're doing what they're doing."

Scott re-addresses Father Mark's tendency to promote God's power to improve one's personal place in life. "Father, one of the things you often talk about is how people can use the power of God and universal energy to improve their position in this world. You even go as far as covering the sensitive topic of using God's power to improve one's success and personal wealth. Is this something a Catholic priest should be talking about?"

With a patient grin, Father Mark continues, "Scott, I believe that spiritual leaders should cover all the topics that are important to people. Financial stability is very important for our society, so why not help people achieve it?"

Scott nods in approval.

"That said, society needs to be disciplined and restrain itself in the pursuit of wealth. An individual should not be a slave to his or her desires and appetites or have too much passion for 'things.'" He raises his hands up and unites the first two fingers on each hand and moves them to represent quotations as he says the word 'things.' "Opulence is ultimately the demise of the individual. In other words, we need to govern ourselves.

"And what would be the source of the power to control one's self? It's in the power of prayer and the power of gratitude. While you may be able to afford this or that expensive item, the self-control one has to not splurge can be peaceful. So, while I share with people that if they tap into their internal power they can achieve great things, I also stress that personal restraint is critical to true happiness."

As the interview proceeds to a close, Scott wants to discuss what Father Mark has planned next for his mission. "So, what's next for you Father? Your voice has been heard and now, through this 60 Minutes broadcast, millions more will have heard it. I suspect that some of your Catholic leaders will not be completely pleased with what I call your liberal approach. How do you move forward? How will you continue for the future?"

Realizing the interview is wrapping up, Father Mark says, "Scott, first I want to thank you and 60 Minutes for having me on your show to share my ideas. Hopefully, this conversation will inspire some of your viewers. I want to thank all those who will watch this interview" Once more Father Mark looks directly into camera #3. "I ask that while you may not agree with all of my perspectives, give them some thought, and maybe try embracing them. Don't judge, just contemplate."

Father Mark then turns away from the camera and looks once again at Scott. "As to what I'm going to do next, I'm going to take a bit of a break. I'm going to suspend my direct activity with the Church and take somewhat of a hiatus."

Scott quickly interrupts, "So, Father, are you saying that your views have caused stress in your relationship with the Catholic Church and you need to step down from being an active priest?"

"Let me say this," Father Mark responds, "there certainly has been some stress created, and we can all understand that. I'm one hundred percent fine with it. But this decision to step away has been going through my mind for some time, and I'm not saying I'm leaving the Catholic Church, but the voice inside of me, I believe God's voice, is guiding me.

"Here's what my plan is … over the next few days I'll be leaving the country and taking the Camino Pilgrimage in northern Spain. The Camino Pilgrimage is also known as Camino de Santiago or the Way of Saint James. I will walk along the path of the Way of Saint James, a blend of walking and riding with guides, to do some soul-searching and writing.

"For those who don't know about this trail, it became one of the most important Christian pilgrimages during the latter part of the Middle Ages. Legend holds it that St. James's remains were carried by boat from Jerusalem to northern Spain where he was buried in what is now the city of Santiago de Compostela. Today, people from around the world take this pilgrimage walk to move deeper into spirituality, get closer to God, and maybe even find their true meaning. For me, it will be the opportunity to do the same and also to write."

Scott asks, "What will you be writing?"

Father Mark's huge smile reflects his inner peace with his decision. "A friend of mine has been trying to convince me to write a book of some kind. He tells me that my ideas have been greatly resonating with many people and, if I decided to write a book about my ideas, I could help even more people. I don't know if he's correct, but if he's watching, he knows he's going to be busy helping me get my ideas to paper.

"We'll see how this turns out. I'm going to be at peace as I experience the beauty of the Camino Pilgrimage, and I'll take what God says to me, and I'll put those ideas on paper. Maybe it will never get published, and it will just be something for me to have. I'll leave that to the publishers to decide. After spending several months on this journey, I will then decide what is next for me and my life."

"Father Mark, I can tell you this, if you publish any kind of book, I for one will read it. I suspect millions more will do the same." Then what is not commonly done after a 60 Minutes interview takes place, Scott Pelley stands up and says, "Father I want to thank you for coming and doing this interview."

Father Mark stands up as well not knowing what will happen next. Scott steps closer to Father Mark and embraces him with a hug. Father Mark returns the embrace, and they remain this way for a few seconds.

As Father Mark and Scott Pelley separate from their embrace, the director yells "CUT" to indicate the cameras can stop rolling. Scott then puts his right hand on Father Mark's left shoulder and says, "Father, I want to thank you again. What a great interview. Go write that book and inspire us all."

Five Months Later

Over the last five months, Father Mark experiences his pilgrimage at the Camino de Santiago … the Way of Saint James. The pilgrimage usually takes between thirty and thirty-five days, but Father Mark spends many days and weeks exploring the villages, towns, and meeting people along the Camino path, often spending several nights in remote areas with his sleeping quarters varying between a tent, a villager's home, modest inns and, at times, under the stars in his sleeping bag.

With his backpack lightly stocked—a small Apple MacBook computer, a cell phone that he hardly turned on, a large water bottle, a few extra shirts, shorts, socks, spare pants, and an extra pair of hiking shoes, he endures hot days and cool nights. He walks many miles alone enjoying the beautiful landscape of northern Spain while praying, meditating, and listening to his inner voice.

He meets other brave pilgrims and, together, they share life stories, fears, and prayers. The villagers he meets enjoy a simple life. They love the land and God. Many are Catholic but not all. Father Mark spends time sharing ideas and views with many of them. They laugh and cry together. He meets so many wonderful people from all walks of life. He truly enjoys their company. He equally enjoys his alone time. Sometimes he suffers greatly when he thinks about his lost family and how his journey took him to this pilgrimage.

At times, Father Mark feels confused as to why God chose this path for him, why he had to suffer the loss of his family, and why he is chosen to bring unpopular ideas to the followers of the Catholic Church. He transitions between joy and sadness often, but always keeps his faith in God. He often repeats to himself one of his favorite verses from the Bible: *Lean not on your own understanding.* He knows he can't completely understand the intentions of God, but he keeps his faith that God is guiding him, and he accepts this guidance.

Each day, he writes the ideas that come to his mind. He prays to God, asking for guidance and inspiration for ideas that will inspire people—ideas that can help people live a more fulfilling and happier life. Some days the ideas flood in and other days his mind rests quietly. He decides to write his ideas in a way that will be short inspirations. He wants the inspirations to be written so that people read and focus on only one per day. He wants to have his readers execute one inspiration a day to create one single day of peace at a time.

Every few weeks when Father Mark finds an Internet connection, he emails his writings to Jonathan. Jonathan writes back inquiring how Father Mark is feeling, his whereabouts, and when he plans to return. Father Mark answers each of Jonathan's emails with a short response of "I'm fine, all good. Thank you for helping me write our book. God bless." He never mentions when he will return.

As Father Mark approaches the end of the Way of Saint James, also believed by some as the end of the earth, he is amazed at the beauty of the deep, blue North Atlantic Ocean. He walks past a ceramic scallop shell affixed to a cement pillar designed to confirm to those on this journey that they have arrived. This is the final scallop shell marker. All along his journey of the Camino, the Scallop Shell is used as a symbol of direction, pointing pilgrims towards Santiago. Father Mark sees many pilgrims wearing this symbol as a decorative necklace, attached to their back backs, or worn somewhere on their body. This further enhances the camaraderie. Everyone knows their fellow pilgrims on the Camino journey.

The Scallop Shell has a significant meaning on the Camino, the Walk of Saint James. Saint James worked as a fisherman alongside his brother, John, before becoming a disciple of Christ. Following the death and resurrection of Jesus, the apostles began to spread the gospel and convert others to Christianity. As part of his mission, James travelled to Iberia, landing at present-day town of Padron, to preach to pagans in the area. Sadly, on his return to Jerusalem he was beheaded by King Herod for blasphemy.

Following his execution, James' headless body had been brought to Galicia in northwest Spain to be laid to rest. Here's where the Scallop Shell comes in. There are two versions as to what took place from this point on. The first is, off the coast of Spain, a heavy storm hit the ship and St. James' body became lost in the ocean. After some time, however, it washed to the shore undamaged and covered in scallops. The second version is that after James's death, his body had been transported by a ship piloted by an angel to be buried in what is now Santiago. As the ship approached land, a wedding celebration took place on the shore. The young groom was riding on horseback and, seeing the ship approaching, his horse became frightened, and both horse and rider plunged into the sea. Through a miraculous intervention, the horse and the rider emerged from the water alive, covered in scallop shells.

Father Mark walks to the stone cross statue sitting high on top of an immense boulder at the very end of the Camino. Beyond the stone cross appears the beautiful blue sea. Father Mark always loves being by the sea, but this view could be the most magnificent and calming he has ever experienced. The sea stretched as far as the eye could see. His five-month prolonged journey had come to an end. As he stares at the ocean, Father Mark wonders what is next for him. He says out loud to himself something he counseled many people about who became saddened by something ending in their life: "Every ending has a new beginning."

Father Mark knows there will be more new and interesting things to take place in his life. At this moment, he just doesn't know what they might be.

He shakes himself out of this pleasurable trance and realizes he has one more very important objective. Now that he has come to the end of the Camino, he needs to send his final writings to Jonathan.

Back in New Jersey, Jonathan waits daily in great anticipation for emails from Father Mark. Each email has Father Mark's most recent writings, and he starts every one with the title: More Mental Vitamins. What Father Mark calls "mental vitamins" are philosophies and ideas he feels people should embrace and execute on a daily basis. They are concepts that, if implemented, can help people live happier and more successful lives. Some are very simple and well-known ideas. But, while potentially already known, they function as an important reminder. The way Father Mark articulates them has a profound impression on Jonathan.

Jonathan loves tabulating, correlating, and organizing all of the writings. He knows without any doubt that the publishing of Father Mark's writings will make for a hugely successful book. This is exactly what Jonathan had in mind when, many months ago, he recommended to Father Mark that he put his inspirations in writing. The only thing that is perplexing him is the title of the book. He just can't come up with something that is compelling enough. To be great, a title has to be short but impactful. It needs to represent exactly the book's theme, but it shouldn't tell too much. Jonathan keeps his faith that he will be inspired with a great title.

Some weeks pass without any communication from Father Mark. These weeks feel like months to Jonathan. He enjoyed receiving Father Mark's emails and, when too much time elapsed without a communication, Jonathan worries for him. Is he healthy? Is he safe? These and other questions constantly navigate through Jonathan's mind. Then an email would arrive and Jonathan would be relieved. He takes Father Mark's writings and massages the ideas, smoothes out some of the wording, making minor tweaks.

Leaving the end of the Camino Trail, Father Mark strolls into the town of Santiago de Compostela in the province of Galicia. A warm breeze comforts him. His walk has an objective. He has his final writings which he needs to send to Jonathan, so he begins looking for a café or hotel that has an Internet connection. He comes upon a modest hotel, a beautiful stone structure. The magnificent building looks as though it has been there for hundreds of years, yet it seems fresh and new. Father Mark stands outside the hotel and marvels at the beauty. As the sun reflects off the stone, it gives the building a pale orange color, similar to the color of a beautiful sunset.

Father Mark walks up seven steps as his feet wobble between the uneven stones. He arrives at an aged, dark brown wooden door about eight feet high. Opening it, he enters the foyer of the hotel. He feels the cool breeze of an air-conditioned room. A refreshing sensation enters his body. He moves straight ahead to the front desk and, as he looks to the right, he sees a café. He detours to his right and crosses the faded, white marble floor to the café. He greets a young Spanish woman at the hostess desk, "My dear, do you speak English?"

"Yes, Senor, I do. May I help you?"

"Do you have Internet here in the hotel or inside the restaurant?"

"Yes, Senor we do. Would you like a table?"

"Yes, thank you very much."

The hostess takes a menu from her desk and he follows her towards a table by the window on the far side of the café. "Is this okay for you?"

"Absolutely perfect. Gracias." Father Mark gives her a warm smile.

As he sits down, a waiter quickly approaches and says politely, "Senor, may I get you anything to drink?"

"May I have a glass of water with lemon and a cup of coffee please?"

"Certainly, Senor."

"Senor, excuse me" Father Mark adds, "I'm going to get on your Internet. Is there a password?"

"Yes Senor. The password is Camino, C-A-M-I-N-O. Camino. All large letters."

"Of course, it is," smiles Father Mark.

He opens up his backpack and slips out his MacBook Air. He clicks on the Wi-Fi icon at the top right area of the screen and selects the hotel's Internet. He slowly types C-A-M-I-N-O. The connection is successful, he accesses his Gmail account and begins …

Jonathan, I hope you are well. I'm pleased to report that I have reached the end of the Earth. Today, I have completed the Camino Trail, and I've come to one of the most beautiful places I have ever seen. My journey has been long and fulfilling meeting so many wonderful travelers and locals. It delivered all the spirituality I expected it would. Words cannot explain the joy and positive energy I received on this journey.

Where I will go from here, I do not know as of yet. God will guide me, and I will be in touch.

Until then, I'm sending you my final writings for our book. I thank you for being such a loyal friend and for taking your precious time to work with my writings and make sense of them. I'm looking forward to reading the final version when you have it completed.

My one request is that I would like to select the title. You can create any subtitle you would like, and I trust you will author it properly. From here, it is now up to you to complete the writing and contact your publishing friends. I hope your time has not gone to waste, and I hope someone is willing to publish our work. Whatever you think is best regarding the publisher to select as well as the financial arrangement, is what you should do. I trust one hundred percent that you will make the right decisions. We will split any earnings 50/50 (assuming someone will purchase our book!). We don't need any complicated partnership contract. This email will do if you are in agreement. A virtual handshake is all I need.

Again, I thank you. For now, I bid you farewell, and I will be in touch soon.

The title of the book shall be – A Single Day of Peace

See the attached as my final writings. God Bless.

Chapter 17

Jonathan Crew is having trouble sleeping and, as he looks at the digital clock on his TV cable box, it reads 3:46 a.m. Tired of tossing and turning, he gingerly slides to the edge of the bed and gets up quietly so as to not wake his wife. He walks into his office, which is adjacent to his bedroom. He sits down at his desk, opens the laptop computer, sits comfortably, and opens his email. He experiences a delightful sensation seeing an email from Father Mark.

As he reads the email, he becomes saddened and relieved—sad that Father Mark did not confirm when he would be in touch or where he would be going. Jonathan doesn't like not knowing, but he also knows this is how things proceed with Father Mark. Relief sets in that Father Mark has selected the book's title.

Jonathan reacts joyfully to the choice of *A Single Day of Peace*. "That is PERFECT!" he says aloud. He leans back in his black leather swivel chair and puts his hands on his head. A pleased smile forms on his lips. It all comes together perfectly. The title is exactly what Jonathan strived for, and all along it had been right there in front of him. Father Mark uses the phrase "a single day of peace" often. Jonathan loves it. Now he has to come up with the subtitle. Enthusiastically, he begins writing various versions, adjusting and moving words around as if arranging pieces to a jigsaw puzzle. Then, after about twenty minutes, a broad smile lights up his face.

50 Principles That Can Transform Your Life.

Business Leader Turned Controversial Catholic Priest Inspires Millions by Challenging Traditions.

Father Mark Tossi

Introduction by Jonathan Crew

Your Improved Life Starts Today

I, Jonathan Crew, a journalist, have the honor of bringing to you the inspiring principles authored by Father Mark Tossi. Father Mark Tossi created these success principles during his pilgrimage and spiritual journey along the Way of St. James (Camino de Santiago). During this journey, he prayed, meditated, reviewed his life experiences, and asked for divine guidance as to what we need to make our lives more satisfying. He prayed for this guidance so that he could provide humanity with ideas they can implement to make their lives more meaningful, happy, and successful. Many who experience the pilgrimage of the Camino find deep peace and personal guidance. The participation of the Camino de Santiago is a deep spiritual experience that millions have claimed to be a life-changing event. The same is true for Father Mark.

During his journey, Father Mark wrote daily, as he received ideas and divine guidance. He blended the divine guidance with his own experiences to create the daily inspirational principles that follow. As he completed each of his writings, he emailed them to me for refinement. I'm pleased to report that my contribution has been minor, as I smoothed out some of his expressions to simplify comprehension. All of the ideas and philosophies are those of Father Mark Tossi, and none are from me. I am merely an assistant to bring the words to you.

These daily lessons from Father Mark will provide you with proven ways you can transform yourself to improve the happiness and success of your life. The principles Father Mark authored come from over thirty years of personal practice and observation, from his own personal successes, challenges, and the many experiences of those with whom he has interacted. These principles provide you with a fast path to enlightenment and happiness. If you follow these principles, you will no longer have to experience the strenuous process of trial and error to learn the way of a blessed life. This is your shortcut to the critical knowledge you need. All you have to do is take action and implement it.

Many of these insights and experiences come from Father Mark's two lives. The first was as a happily married man, father of two children, and a successful executive leading thousands of employees. He achieved financial independence with a prosperous life. Then it all changed.

After a tragic life event where he lost his entire family, he fell into deep depression and desperation. He broke out of that very dark place and transitioned his life to become a Catholic priest. Living as a husband, father, successful businessperson, and then as a Catholic priest, he has experiences and observations few others have had. He has person- ally failed and succeeded, won and lost, accumulated wealth, mentored many and, as a priest, has witnessed how many are strong but many are weak when it comes to their spirituality. Having counseled many with minor and enormous life challenges, he has the rare perspective on how and why people experience failure, and how they can lift them- selves out of their challenges and prevail.

If you are already very successful but have parts of your life that you're not happy with, these principles will guide you. If you feel you have reached rock bottom and you're desperate for help to save your life, the guidance you receive from these principles can renew you. If you are somewhere in-between, you will surely receive guidance to take your life to the next level of happiness and success.

You can implement these principles and thought-provoking inspirations regardless of your age, gender, education, profession, level of success, status, race, religion, or spiritual beliefs to achieve more happiness and fulfillment. They are a blend of spiritual guidance and successful principles that will motivate you to transform you to your better self.

Each principle of well-being and life success is written to be implemented one per day. Many of the topics will be familiar to you. The question is, have you ever internalized them? Have you made them a part of your daily conscious thoughts and actions? It is one thing to know the idea of a principle; it is a completely different thing to make it a per- manent part of you. Now you will.

Inside of you is a more interesting, powerful, energetic self that can achieve great things while being spiritually balanced. Through demonstrating spiritual leadership, along with disciplined, tough-minded actions, you can be more than you have thought you can be.

We are—and become—the thoughts we think. This being a universal truth, these principles allow you to supplement your mind and your thinking with the ideas that will make your life more successful and happier.

I reiterate, that to get the most out of these writings, you are asked to read and implement only one per day. You are asked to read your daily inspiration when you rise in the morning, sometime during the day, and again before you go off to sleep for your nightly rest. Each reading takes only a few minutes, so time should not be an issue.

You are asked to think about each principle throughout the day. Find a way to implement the principle in some way. Keep it in your conscious thoughts throughout the day. Then, before you go off to sleep at night, read the principle again so that it can stay in your mind throughout the night and become a deep part of your conscious and subconscious mind.

Doing this every day will give you a single day of peace while you grow into a more enlightened and successful person. A key part of having these principles work for you is to take action. You must act and, in some way, implement each of the daily principles.

After you have completed all the readings, you can go back and use this book as a guide to focus on the principles you feel are best for you. As with any instruction and training, repetition is very important. After your first reading,, read the principles as many times as you can and continue to implement the ideas. Doing so will give you more positive energy, a stronger spirit, help you overcome life's challenges, and help you achieve the success you desire, all the while guiding you to be an important part of making this world a better place to live. Today we begin.

Day 1—*Self Esteem – Celebrate Your Difference*

Your new and improved life starts with the recognition that you are a super special human being. Regardless of what you have been—positive or negative, healthy or ill, generous or selfish, happy or sad, successful or a failure—you are a human being who came into this world with special talents.

In the history of humanity, no one has been created exactly like you. Think about that. No one has ever been like you. You are the rarest of all species put on this Earth. Each of us is brought here by the power of God to live a happy and successful life. Each one of us is a great miracle capable of reaching the stars.

Today, you start reminding yourself of your special uniqueness. Today, you begin the creation of the new you. How do you do this? It starts with celebrating who you are and your differences. Too often we look at our differences and see them as a problem or a limitation. Your differences can be the thing that makes you great. Celebrate your differences.

So many happy and successful people had a feeling of inferiority at one time, because those around them made them feel that way. Maybe they thought they were too short, tall, skinny, heavy, had an accent, a speaking lisp, loved music, or saw themselves as less than brilliant ... and then, in time, they realized that who they have been is what has made them special. Look at your differences and embrace them. Remember this: every room you walk into is better because you entered it.

Next, use positive motivating statements and simply say to yourself, "I am great, positive, special, and capable of doing amazing things. God makes no mistakes, and I am no exception. If my life has not been all I wanted it to be, it's because of the decisions I have made and actions I have taken."

It may have also been that those who are closest to you (family, friends, coworkers, etc.) had good intentions but limited your view of yourself. This happens more often than we care to admit. In their love for you, they didn't want you to take risks and possibly be let down, face adversity, or potentially have a short-term setback. Candidly, there are some situations where others just don't want to see you in a better place than they are, so they knock you down.

Today that stops. Today you recognize that you will, in time, make many corrections and become the person who has been inside of you, who is aching to get out. You will achieve this one step at a time, but it starts with you knowing you are great. It starts today.

Believe in yourself because the miracle of God created you. You are put on this Earth capable of climbing the highest mountain, not to be destined to be limited to minor feats. You have unlimited potential, but the problem has been that you haven't used your uniqueness to its fullest. Hence, you become "rusty" and soft.

Today, we dust off that rust and begin anew. Today and every day forward, you will remind yourself that you are unique, special, and powerful. It doesn't matter if you are tall or short, thin or full-bodied, bald or blessed with a full head of hair, grew up in the slums or in riches, young or old, black or white, highly educated or with limited education.

What matters is that God is in you and you are special. While you are a fantastic creation, the goal is not to be perfect. There is no perfection. Too many people put the burden of perfection on themselves. We must understand that perfection is unachievable.

Success in life is not about being perfect. Look at all the great achievers in all walks of life, including athletes, spiritual leaders, business leaders, teachers, mentors, parents, students, etc. They have all stumbled at times.

Perfection is not the way. Know yourself and realize you will err from time to time. That should not negatively impact your self-esteem and positive beliefs. You will learn about positive self-suggestions, and these will be the programing to transform you into someone with enormous self-belief and positive self-esteem. Belief in yourself is the beginning and necessity of creating a new life. You have begun.

Day 2 — *You Can Always Start Anew*

It's never too late to start creating a happier, healthier, and more successful you. If you have just one last day on this Earth, it can be more fulfilling if you change just one thing ... your attitude. Fortunately, for most of us, we have many months and years left on this Earth. So, if we start today, we can have a more fulfilling life for all our remaining days, weeks, months, and years.

History is full of stories of how people late in life made the decision to change and took the appropriate actions to make that change a reality. They then created miracles in their lives. They stopped drinking, quit drugs, became a more patient spouse, a more supportive friend, a better parent, accumulated wealth, created inventions that make our lives more pleasant, overcame life-threatening illnesses, or became world champion athletes. This proves it is never too late to start your new life.

If you start today, you are on your way to greatness one small step at a time. Remember, great things are achieved by taking small moves in the right direction. To start anew, you will have to knock down mental and spiritual walls that have been barriers. You need to take a candid look at any negative energy you are putting out into the Universe and stop immediately.

Don't wait until tomorrow. Those who constantly struggle through life always look to tomorrow to get started. Tomorrow never comes. Be a miracle maker and start today and stick with it. Doing this will change your future, and then you can look back and praise yourself for the courage and commitment you demonstrated for changing your life.

Let yesterday be yesterday. Yesterday is like ashes in a fireplace. They cannot make a new fire today. Many people have a difficult time letting go of yesterday and both the achievements and failures they experienced. Equally self-poisoning is the individual who constantly reminisces their successes of yesterday while not making changes for a better today and tomorrow, as is the person who continues to mourn over past defeats.

*Recognize and feel good about your past successes and make more today. Forget your sins and bad breaks of days gone by and create new greatness today. As you start your new you, follow your heart. What are you passionate about? What is it you always wanted to do? The best **you** is the person who pursues the true desires of your heart. Doing things out of obligation deteriorates your spirit. We all have obligations we must meet and that is part of living a responsible life; but if you're only doing the things that you're obli-*

134

gated to do, your spirit will suffer. Go after what you're passionate about and do what you love.

Day 3 — *Our Belief System*

We are all a product of our beliefs. Our actions, reactions, decisions, judgments, opinions, behaviors, and preferences are all driven by our beliefs. Today, take inventory of your beliefs. Take the time to inspect the approximate 60,000 thoughts that go through your mind today and acknowledge your ingrained beliefs.

Do you believe people are inherently good or evil? Do you believe it is not right that some people have extreme wealth? Do you believe in God? Do you believe that we should take better care of the homeless? Do you believe that envy of others and the things they possess is not healthy? Do you believe you have a powerful spirit inside of you?

Do you believe ... education is important, in life after death, that it is dangerous to park your car in a middle-class neighborhood, that you should work hard, set goals, that it is unsafe to live in a large city, that you don't need to learn from motivational or spiritual leaders, that you shouldn't trust people, that you should be suspicious of people you do business with, that your boss has your best interests in mind, that you can be financially independent, that we should give to the poor, that the police are a threat, drinking alcohol every day won't hurt your health, talking down to your spouse or partner is acceptable, while you don't have children you have all the answers to effective parenting, it's better to be a nonconformist, we should treat all animals with respect, diversity is important, you should eat healthy, you should exercise, people of a different race are inferior, or you should not eat meat? Do you believe that you are a spiritual being using your body while here on this Earth, or that you can manifest what you want in this life?

You get the idea ... we all have thousands of deeply ingrained beliefs. If you are going to change and improve your life, you have to be honest with yourself as to what your beliefs are and question those that are holding you back.

This is one of the most difficult things for people to do. Why? Because if you look yourself honestly in the mirror and question the beliefs you've had for a long time, it makes you vulnerable. You are vulnerable, because you may have to admit you've been "wrong" about some things. You have to admit that some of your beliefs have limited you.

Now the growth begins! Within the willingness to be vulnerable is the seed of progress. As your beliefs drive your behavior, you must adjust the limiting and fearful beliefs, so you can behave and act differently. Put your ego aside and be honest with yourself. The daily inspirations you will read and, hopefully, put into practice, will challenge and influence your beliefs.

Most people who struggle with their lives have belief systems that are limiting and self-defeating. They have excuses for their challenges and see the outside world as the culprit of their situation. I'm encouraging you to stop looking outside yourself, to look deeply inside, and take personal responsibility for what you have chosen to believe.

Many of our beliefs developed during our upbringing and how our parents and/or caregivers have influenced us. While most of our parents meant well, often the beliefs they instilled limited us. They instilled only what they knew. If you want more than they achieved, you have to instill new and additional beliefs.

Did your parents, teachers, coaches, relatives, friends, mentors, bosses, the books you read, your personal experiences, or your religious upbringing instill in you that you can achieve great things, that you have a powerful spirit inside of you, that you should love your neighbor, that you should show respect for others? Or did they instill in you caution, status climbing, suspicion, cheating to get ahead, skepticism, fear, or other limiting ideas? New, additional, and adjusted beliefs will be the catalyst to thinking and behaving differently. These new behaviors will be your action to create the world you want for yourself. Take honest inventory of your beliefs and assess if they are limiting you. Be vulnerable and grow.

Day 4 — *Your Thoughts Create Your Destiny*

You become what you think about most. Period. The thoughts you think direct your life … positive or negative. Change your thoughts and the words you speak to yourself and you will change your life. This is the universal secret that too few have learned. Life is a self-fulfilling prophecy. You are and become what you think about most.

In essence, you are a programmable computer. What you put IN you get OUT. If you put negative thoughts in, you get a life of challenges and disappointments. If you put positive and aspirational thoughts in, your life magically improves, and positive things happen.

It doesn't happen overnight; it happens a little bit at a time. The way you program yourself for success and happiness is by creating self-suggestions of what you want to continue to be and become. The key secret is to create the self-suggestions in the present tense starting with "I am" versus "I will be."

Self-suggestions must be written down. There is something spiritual about writing them down and having them close to you at all times. Write them down and put them in your purse or your wallet, so you can take them out to read them several times a day. Put them into your smart phone, so you can pull them up several times a day and read them. Reading them several times a day allows you to program yourself often.

If you want to be a more patient parent, here's what you write: "I am a calm and patient mother/father. When stressful things happen with my children or they misbehave, I stay very calm and thoughtful."

If you want to be more persistent, write: "I am respectfully persistent when I want to accomplish something. As I collaborate with others, I stay strong in my direction and, while I'm open to other's views, I don't back down when I want to achieve something."

If you want to be healthier and lose weight, write: "I make good eating decisions and make sure that I stay away from snacks, candy, and all unhealthy foods. I often eat lean protein and vegetables. I work out three to five times a week, and I weigh _____ (put in the weight you want to be)."

Transforming your thoughts in this way controls your actions. When you go off track and behave differently from your new self-suggestions, you will be instantly reminded of the new you, and you will adjust. You will stop the old behavior and execute the new behavior. There are many books about this, and I encourage you to find one that resonates with you and read it. Probably the most impactful one I ever read is Think and Grow Rich *by Napoleon Hill. The word "rich" does not only mean riches in the form of money but any of this world's "riches" you want to attract. We become what we think about most. Program yourself and your life in the direction you want to become.*

Day 5 — *Connect with Your Inner Spirit - The Higher Power*

We are all spiritual beings having a human experience. Think about this. Think deeply about this. You are, in essence, your spirit. While you're on this Earth, you have a body that your spirit resides in, but you are not your body. You are your spirit. Most people will say that they never thought of themselves in this way. When you do, your life changes for the better. We are all spirits moving through this world. When you see others—your friends, family members, co-workers, or passers-by on the street—look at them as their spirit. What spirit are they projecting?

Think of yourself as a spiritual being having a human experience in your body. If you can grasp this idea, you will begin to recognize the power you have to create the life you want—a fulfilled and happy life. Your spirit is what seeks goodness and knows there is hope in the midst of challenges and despair. It is the positive part of you that, when things are going well, reminds you to be thankful and have gratitude.

This is the part of you that speaks to you like that little voice inside that tells you there is something much more and greater out there for you. Your spirit is what is closest to God, and that is why it constantly whispers into your ear that there are greater things in store for you, and you can become that self-actualized person you want to be.

A part of spiritual leadership is the process of reminding others of their inner spirit to encourage them during their successful or challenging times, and that they can rely on this spirit for guidance.

Another part of spiritual leadership is respecting the spirit of others. The term Namaste, often heard in Yoga classes, is the acknowledgement and respect shown to another's spirit. It is the respect and reverence of others. It is honoring others, being appreciative of others. It is also recognizing we are all One. It is a way to recognize others with more of a God-conscious attitude than with your ego. We are not better. We are One. We are together.

The spirit inside of you is what gives you unlimited potential. This is what Jesus meant when he told the people "you can do even greater things than these." Everyone is spiritual but not everyone taps into their spiritual being. It is simple to do. Just acknowledge that God is in you, and you will connect with that God power and awaken your spirit.

140

Keep thinking and reminding yourself of the spirit that you are, and you will feel and see changes in your life. Your spirit will come out in many ways. You will be more patient, more relaxed, more confident, make better business and personal decisions, and you will be more aware of what is going on around you. Your intuition will improve, you will be more loving and attract more love, positive things will come into your life, and you will be more inspired and happier.

Day 6 — *Set Goals*

You have to chart your course in life in order to get to the place you want to be. Otherwise, you'll drift like a stranded boat out at sea. Show me someone who is a great parent, a successful student, a successful business person, a self-made wealthy person, a successful actress, someone who is fit and in good health, who is spiritually sound, an amazing teacher, a fantastic doctor ... you name the category ... and I will show you someone who has set and committed to great goals--goals that are important to them.

There is a very important aspect to setting goals. You will put in the effort to achieve your goals if they bring you intrinsic satisfaction and a result you deeply desire. This is why goals/objectives set by others, such as your boss, your parents, your spouse, your company, your sales leader, etc., don't inspire you, and you probably don't achieve them.

There is a positive scientific process that goes on inside of you that creates joy when you pursue your interests and your goals. These goals bring you intrinsic rewards, and that is the inspiration that drives you to achieve YOUR goals. People who set goals are very clear about the "why" of their goals. The "why" of your goals is very important to define. Doing this will give you more clarity and focus to achieve your goals.

A goal is the fuel that drives your behavior. Plain and simple, without goals, you wallow in and are at the whim of infrequent successes that happen to come your way. What do you want to have or be in the next three, six, nine, or twelve months? What do you want your life to be like in five or ten years?

Think long and hard about it, and then write down your goals and put a plan together to achieve them. Do you want to be a certain weight, run a marathon, save a specific amount of money, travel to a new country, be president of a company, start your own business, improve your marriage, create a charity, close more businesses, have more friends, be more spiritual? Whatever motivates you, you can and will achieve what you want if you set goals and commit to them.

Before you set out to achieve success, first define what success is to you. This is very important. Every one of us has a different definition of success for ourselves. Define yours. Once you decide what goals motivate you, believe BIG and pray BIG.

The best definition of success is the pursuit of a worthwhile goal. If you're pursuing something positive, you're a success. If you're not, you're wallowing. If you use your spirit with positive intentions and pray to your higher power, there is no goal too big.

142

Be bold. There are five keys to successfully setting goals.

(1) *Your goals must be very specific. What is the specific amount of money you want to save or earn, what is the exact weight you want to be, how many spiritual readings do you want to read each day, what kind of yoga studio do you want to open, what is the exact marathon you want to run? Be very specific.*

(2) *Goals must have a specific timeframe and date you will achieve them. By defining a specific date, you engage your spirit, your conscious mind, and your subconscious mind to achieve the goal in the specified time. You also engage the Universe to help you get to where you want to be by a specific date.*

(3) *The goal must be something you really, really, really want. If it's just a "nice to have," you will fold when you face the slightest adversity, and you will give up on it. But, if it is life or death for you, something you deeply desire, you will put forward the effort and fight and display grit to achieve it.*

(4) *Your goals must be repeated every day. Better yet, multiple times each day while you see yourself already achieving the goal. This is self-programing.*

(5) *Your goals must be in writing. You can write/type your goals on paper or store them digitally in your smart phone. It doesn't matter where you write them; what matters is you get them written. This makes you take the time to think and commit to them. Your goals are what make you the new you. Set them and commit to them. Nothing is more satisfying than achieving a goal and the feeling of "I did it!!" That said, when you get in the habit of setting and achieving goals, you will learn that happiness comes in the pursuit of the goal versus the achievement of it. Don't get me wrong, achieving your goal will be a great feeling, but the worthwhile pursuit of the goal sets your energy on a new path, and you'll be amazed how good you feel as you go after it. So, go and experience it.*

Day 7 — *Do Something Wonderful for Someone*

When you do something positive for others, you create positive energy and that boomerangs back to you. If you seek happiness for others, you will find it for yourself. Making the world a better place for someone makes your world better. The intent of your good should be to solely do something positive for someone else, not for self-gain. When you demonstrate this, via the natural energy of the Universe, you make your life better.

Some of the greatest things you can do for others is to encourage them, believe in them, show them love, give them your full attention, connect with them, or send them inspiring messages. Find a charity you believe in and join it, support it, or donate to it. Maybe you saw a great inspiring video on YouTube, and you forwarded it to someone you know who needs that message or will be further inspired by it.

Be the source of positivity. Be the source of possibility thinking. Be the person who is just there for someone who needs it today. When you do good things for others, your world improves. The opposite is true as well. Every time we express negative words or thoughts at someone, we're hurting ourselves.

Every time you judge someone, it is a reflection of how you're judging yourself. Thou shall not judge is a powerful Bible statement. If we judge others, we will be judged. Being negative and judgmental of others is the work of our ego. Our ego can be very detrimental to us.

If you need to be better, faster, wealthier, healthier, smarter, or more accomplished than others, this creates significant negative vibes within you. When someone outshines you, recognize when your ego jumps in with negative thoughts and stop those thoughts. Replace them with good feelings for that person, and you will have good come to you. Do something small or great but do something positive for someone else today.

Day 8 — *Be Calm*

We must learn to relax and be calm. Anything we do in life, we do better if we're calm. Rest your spirit, your body, and your mind. Monitor how many things you are trying to do at once. Monitor your rate of speech. Monitor the pace of what is going on inside of you. If it's all going too quickly, find a quiet place, close your eyes, take deep breaths, and see yourself as being calm.

Picture yourself in the scene of one of your favorite places: a tropical beach, in the mountains, at the red rocks in Arizona, anywhere that helps you feel peaceful and calm. Being calm is like being in the zone that athletes talk about. Being in the zone isn't just for athletes, it's for all of us. A parent who is calm and, in the zone, creates a calmer and more confident child, a business leader who stays calm when things are going wrong creates confident employees, a friend who gives the energy of peace to another who is upset helps them get to a better place faster.

Smile often today and look at everything in a positive way. Send positive energy to everyone you see. Today, constantly tell yourself you are calm. By the end of the day, you will have a unique feeling of relaxation and joy.

Day 9 — *Embrace the Winds of Change*

Change makes most people uncomfortable, because it takes away the familiar. But in change is the sea of newness and adventure—new people, new relationships, new challenges, or new beliefs. Change helps you transform to the new you. There will be uncertainty but, if you persevere with a positive attitude, you'll be reborn to new experiences.

That is one of the main purposes of life: to experience. Change takes you out of your comfort zone. Too often, you get into a rut staying with what you know when deep down you're not satisfied with your current situation. Getting out of your comfort zone challenges you, but when you step into the unchartered waters and see it through, more often than not the new experience is very rewarding, and you embrace the new you.

To transform to a better, stronger, and happier "you" requires that you to force new things into your life. Life will always throw changes at you. You will often greet this with frustration. Instead, be open to it, and ask the higher powers why this is happening and what is meant for you by this change. Have faith that the change will bring you more positive things in your life and, with this attitude, you will see new and exciting things come into your life.

Some change requires very difficult decisions and short- to medium-term pain. Ending a relationship, changing jobs, moving to a new state or country, putting distance between yourself and some of your friends, starting a new relationship, finally having that candid conversation with a friend or loved one—all of these require courage to execute, and they will bring on change in your life.

But, without experiencing that pain and getting through it, you will never find the new you. Just ask the woman who is happily married for twenty-five years after she broke away from a previous unfulfilling relationship. Or, ask the man or woman who is working their dream job after a very painful decision to leave a secure position, or the musician who is meeting her goals but had to leave a previous band to go her own way. Our world is full of examples of people who had the courage to face their current situation, decided to change, executed the change, experienced pain, and then fought through the pain to glory. You can, too. Every ending has a new beginning.

Day 10 — *Embrace Others as They Are*

Sometimes, one of the most difficult daily things we have to do is collaborate with others. Everyone is different. We often criticize others for who they are. Those that are closest to us, the ones we love—a spouse, children, partners, friends, relatives, co-workers, neighbors, etc.—we often try to change them for what we think is good for them. In some ways, we may have a clear view of what we feel is good for them, because we're outside looking in. BUT, we must allow them to be free to be who they are. That is love. Coaching and guiding others is great but, at the end of the day, we must embrace all our differences. Who are you trying to change today? Will you embrace who they are?

Day 11 — *It's Okay to Say No*

When it comes to improving your life, what is equally as important as deciding what you want and need to do, is deciding what you are NOT going to do. Part of creating a happier and more fulfilled and spiritual life is your willingness to say "no." Saying no is okay. You don't need to feel guilty if you have to say no to some people as you set your new course in life. Often, this is a big part of moving in a new direction. You have to say no to the old behaviors, habits and, yes, even to some friends.

Successful businesspeople will tell you that some of the most critical decisions they made included deciding what NOT to do. We all try to please too many people. We're afraid of what people will think if we choose not to do what they're asking us to do. If your decisions are based on good intentions and you're trying to make your world and everyone else's a better place to be in, saying no is a positive thing.

Time is all we have, and if we waste it doing too many things, we do very little that makes a positive difference in our lives. If we can teach this to our teenagers, they will be on a faster course to better grades and a healthier lifestyle. Too many high school and college students get off track due to peer pressure. We need to empower them to follow their spirit and have the strength to say no to the things that will distract them from achieving what they want.

Take inventory of what you're doing and what you really don't want to be doing and make a commitment to yourself to adjust and stop doing it. Be respectful in explaining your "no" to others but take that action. The things you decide not to do will set you free.

Day 12 — *Life Is a Learning Process*

If we accept life as a learning process, we'll be more secure in ourselves in that we don't know everything, that we make mistakes, that we're uncertain, that we're scared at times, and that at times we're very correct about things. If we are willing to be open to learning and realize that learning is part of why we are here on Earth, we'll embrace the ups and downs with more happiness and grace. We'll use the learning experiences as a process to get to our best selves.

Patience is a key part of realizing life is a learning process. Patient learning helps you become more peaceful in the process. See your daily ups and downs as the necessary path to your personal greatness. We all want to learn faster and make fewer mistakes. There is a way for you do to that ... ask for help. Seek those people who have done what you want to do and ask for their assistance. Ninety-nine percent of the people who are asked to help are happy to do so.

Part of rolling with the punches of learning life's lessons is not to be so stressed when things don't go the way you want. There is a saying that goes, "You have to care, but not that much." The meaning here is that you have to care but you have to keep the emotions in check if things don't go your way. It is very unhealthy to overly stress when things aren't going as you want. Keep your faith and pray to God and the universal power for wisdom and guidance when things aren't turning out as you planned. When you pray, ask for understanding and learning from the situation. The misses in life teach us. Keep learning from them.

Day 13 — *Work Ethic*

Since the beginning of time, this principle has held true: More has been achieved through hard work than luck. Who your parents are, where you grew up, the schools you went to, or even intelligence—no other attribute or life circumstance is more important than your commitment to working your hardest. Combine hard work with intelligence, and you have superstar potential. But, given a choice of either, I would take hard work over intelligence.

Those who work the hardest, achieve the most. This applies to any walk of life. Work is not your enemy—it is your friend. We all think we would be happier if we didn't have to work and could just live the day as we wanted to. Many people achieve the life dream of early retirement and struggle with boredom. They have no mission in their lives.

See your work as life's oxygen. It keeps you alive spiritually. It gives you purpose. Those who do more of what is asked of them and commit to out-working others receive great rewards. Work ethic is a very interesting topic these days when you blend it with the different perspectives of millennials, gen X's, Y's, and Z's.

Many of today's younger generation tend to have a higher priority on their quality of life versus sacrificing for success and financial gain. I'm not advocating that this is good or bad, I'm just stating what is. If this group or any other age group makes the conscious decision that they want to work less to relax and experience more, then that is the right decision for them.

That said, they must understand the natural law of "what you put in is what you get out." If, however, you have a goal to be the best in your profession, accumulate success, create financial security, progress in your career, make the sports team, be a great parent, or advance rapidly in your chosen field, your work ethic will be the differentiator.

Work ethic cannot be hidden or faked. Those who put the sweat and hard work into their efforts are always recognized for it. It is as obvious as the sun is bright when someone is working hard ... and, when someone is not. There is something special about the energy that comes out of people who are working hard. It is contagious. Hard work is highly valued by the leaders around you, especially when you start a new endeavor such as a new job.

We all must realize that we have to pay the price of success, and that price is hard work. We all start at the bottom, and we have to work our way up. The speed at which you elevate to your desired destination is the amount of the work you put in. If you work really hard, you will move forward from the grunt work everyone must do when they start out.

Your co-workers may not love it, because they see you are different, and you are set-ting a new standard. I encourage you hard workers to bring along the others to join you. If they do, they too will enjoy the pride and progress of the effort. If you want to be success-ful, work harder than the rest. It's that simple.

A work ethic, when not aligned with everyone, is something that can hold back any organization, company, or team. I have advised companies and organizations that had some people working their tail off to progress their mission forward, while others in the same organization took it slow, didn't want to rock the boat, and just wanted to make it easy for themselves. This misalignment killed the culture. The leaders made the mistake of not getting everyone on the same page. They didn't make the decisions consistent with achieving great things. If they weren't interested in being the best, they should just have opened up to it and told everyone in the organization. Assess your work ethic and deter-mine if it's in alignment with your goals.

On this topic, I leave you with this quote— "Ennui: nothing is so intolerable to woman or man as to be completely at rest, without passions, without occupation, without diversion, without work...immediately from the depth of her/his heart will emerge ennui, gloom, sadness, resentment, vexation, despair..." The Pensees, 1654, Blaise Pascal

Day 14 — *What Is Your Slant?*

This is about your intention—what you put out into the world is what, you get back. What is your energy, your slant? What are you projecting out into the world? What energy are you giving others? This is something you must become very conscious about. Your conscious intention creates your world. Have you ever noticed that when you talk to some people they are energized, and their conversation "slant" is optimistic, opportunistic, and has an aura of possibility while others give off a negative vibe? Their intention clearly reflects their mindset and what will come into their lives.

Those who have a negative slant project little statements like, "Yeah, it's sunny, but it's still too cold out," or "Yes, I live by the beach, but it's too crowded," or "The plane's here, but I'm sure they'll find a way to delay us," or "Why does this always happen to me?" They tend to see the limitations in most things.

Here's a story that's a very good example of this. A short time ago, I received an invitation from a CEO of a very successful company to speak to him and his entire management team on the topic of spiritual leadership. Among other things, spiritual leadership is when leaders behave in a way that demonstrates true caring for their people, holds everyone accountable, and enables continuous improvement to optimize employee engagement, satisfaction, and results.

I arrived at the company's offices over an hour early and, instead of sitting in their lobby, I went next door to a Panera Bread shop to get breakfast and coffee. A young lady in her early to mid-twenties worked the counter and took my order. When she asked if she could be of help, her tone indicated that she really wasn't interested in helping me.

She never looked at me as I placed my order, she spoke very softly, as if she didn't care about my presence there, and she had an aura as if the weight of the world sat on her shoulders. She didn't have an ounce of positive energy. It felt like she had an "attitude." I don't know her personal situation, and maybe she did have the weight of the world on her shoulders, but I tried to engage her in conversation asking about her morning, etc. I received uninspired one-word answers.

After my breakfast, I went to the office building to meet the CEO and his staff. Upon arriving at the main lobby, a middle-aged security guard sat behind the main reception desk, and he welcomed me with a huge smile and greeting that could light up a room. He genuinely cared how my morning progressed. After I signed in, he expertly detailed how I would find the office where I would meet the CEO. I don't know this gentleman's situa-

tion in life, but I do know that he is attracting positive things to himself, and the young lady at Panera Bread is not.

The vibe we give the world comes back to us. Scrutinize your behavior and intentions every day ... the thoughts you think and what tone you communicate to others. Do you get uptight quickly when things seem go a bit sideways? Do you see only the challenges around you? Are you often critical of others and the circumstances around you?

If you want to be calmer and more peaceful, change the way you look at things. Dr. Wayne Dyer said it best, "When you change the way you look at things, the things you look at change." This is one hundred percent true. It starts with you, your energy, and your perspective. If you want more peace in your life, give others peace. If you want to be calmer in stressful situations, give calm to others. If you want more confidence to do more with your life, encourage others with confidence. If you want more love, give more love. The thoughts, words, and energy we put out into the world is what we tell the Universe to bring back to us. Life is a self-fulfilling prophecy, so use it to your favor. Be a source of optimism and positive expectancy. If you do, little by little, watch your world change for the better.

Day 15 — *Dealing with Adversity*

Life can be hard. We all have to deal with ups and downs. We all have adversity in our lives. The true fact is, it's not getting knocked down that's the issue (we all get knocked down), it's what we do when we get back up. Get up with determination and the understanding that the stuff that goes on in our lives is just one phase of our lives.

Do your best to stay in an even emotional state—don't get too high when things are going well and don't get too low when you face adversity. All great achievers experience setbacks. You will not be an exception. Know this is the normal process of a successful life. Stay as even as you can throughout the emotional ups and downs.

Embrace adversity; it is a part of the life process. Adversity is actually our friend. Nothing great is ever achieved unless you have overcome adversity. Nothing. So, when you set out to do something great, such as raise a family, start a business, get married, become a millionaire, start a charity, change jobs, play in that big game, etc., I PROMISE you that you will have one or more adversities to deal with. It's a law of nature.

Understanding this changes your world, because when an adversity or a problem hits you, rather than seeing it as evidence that you cannot achieve what you set out to do, you will now recognize it for what it is ... a challenge. It's a challenge that you will overcome by analyzing the situation, thinking through all the information around it, putting a plan together to overcome it, and executing the persistent activities that will overcome it.

Go on the Internet and search something like "people who achieved success after adversity" and you will see story after story of people that had major difficulties that they had to overcome to become who they are today. One of the greatest understandings you can have is knowing that adversity (or multiples of them) is not the signal to tell you that you will not win, that you will not reach your objective, but simply the natural process of what it takes to be successful at what you aim to do. Adversity is your friend and your feedback mechanism. Without it, you will never know the adjustments you need to make to reach your goal.

Day 16 — *Don't Fear Failure*

The word failure creates a significant amount of negative emotions in most people. No one wants to be a failure. No one wants to lose. We are so afraid to fail that often we don't endeavor to do great things, because the pain of standing still is less painful than trying something bold and failing. We are afraid of what everyone will think of us if we fail. We are not sure if our self-esteem can deal with failing. The word failure has such a final sentiment to it.

The critical important point we must understand is that failure is not final. Failure is not permanent. When something doesn't work out, it simply means that you found a way that does not work. Failure is just a feedback mechanism. It is the feedback you need to adjust. That's it! You are NOT a failure—you just found out a way that this particular thing does not work.

Actually, we should take the word failure out of our vocabulary. It has such a negative connotation that it paralyzes people. Rather than the word failure, let's use the phrase "It didn't work." Isn't that less threatening? Less final?

Here's something to think about. Every human-made item that we enjoy on this wonderful Earth had been created through trial and error—the heater that heats your home, the treadmill you run on to stay in shape, the stove you cook on, the TV you watch, the smartphone you use daily—everything you enjoy that had been created by a woman or a man did not come out perfectly the first time around. It went through iterations and iterations of ways it didn't work until, through learning, persistence, and belief, a person or team of people broke through and found a way that it would work.

Without the feedback of what didn't work, one would never get to the point to learn how it would work. With this new perspective, you can now venture out and be bold to try the things you always wanted to do, and you will look forward to learning what doesn't work (not failure) so that you can get to what does.

The interesting thing is the faster you find out what doesn't work, the faster you'll get to what does work and be successful. So, go interview for that new job, start that new business, ask that man out, make that new friendship, make that recommendation to your boss, or go find that long lost family member. And, if it doesn't work out right away, analyze what happened, learn from it, make changes, and try again.

The great professional golfer Greg Norman said it well, "Professional athletes expect to win and respect failure." Keep trying, and you will succeed. Now, tell yourself over and over that failure is not final, it is the critical feedback you need to adjust and move from what didn't work to what will. With that attitude, you will try more things with less anxiety, and you will achieve what you deeply desire.

Day 17 — *We All Mourn*

We all have crossroads in our life. We lose a loved one. We have difficult decisions to make. Do I stay in this marriage or end it? Do I change jobs? Should I move to Europe or stay in North America? Should I go for rehab or keep drinking? Whatever your crossroad is, have peace in that others have them too.

To find the answer you seek, tap into your higher power. Pray, meditate, take a long walk to think, stay silent, or do whatever works for you to get in touch with your inner self. Let God and the Universe speak to you. It probably won't be a thunderous answer but, in short time, your inner voice will guide you. Just be open to the answer and take action.

Losing a loved one to death or separation is probably one of the most difficult experiences we have. No one can provide words of wisdom to make the pain disappear quickly. Only in time does the wound heal. That said, talking and thinking deeply about your emotional pain does truly help.

Praying is a great help. In the case of death, knowing that the spirit of that person has moved on to another place is comforting. I don't know about you, but when loved ones close to me passed on, I looked at their bodies and knew THEY were no longer there. The "they" is their spirit. I look at them and see that their spirit, the essence of them is gone. As I look at their bodies, I recognize their physical presence, but the real them is not there any longer. Hence, I believe we are a spirit moving through a body. Their spirit left their body when that body died.

When I was 16, my brother died after a long battle with cancer. He was 22 years old. This was the first time I experienced the death of someone very close to me. You would think that it would have had a very negative impact on me, but the opposite is true.

Yes, I became very sad, but I equally felt relieved that God had taken him. His long and struggling illness had become very difficult for him, and the time arrived for him to move on to the next life. I remember it as if it was yesterday. I stood in the funeral home as my family received comfort from so many relatives and friends. I stared at my brother lying in that casket, and I felt peace. I knew without any doubt, my brother journeyed somewhere else. His spirit is alive in another place.

That gave me great faith and inner calm. His death awakened my faith that there is life after death. His illness and early death gave me strength. I mourned, but I received strength.

Stephen D'Angelo

In time, your mourning can transform you in the same way. Some mourning is very hard to overcome. The death of young child, a spouse, partner, someone you deeply love. But in time and with faith, you will be healed. You can also go to the people you trust for guidance. One of the things that demonstrates a person's inner strength is their willingness to accept help. Accepting help is not the sign of weakness but the sign of strength. The positive people you are connected with can be a great inspiration and help you through your difficult times. Pick the people who offer positive energy and genuine intention. This is also a reminder for you to help others when they're in need. Be there for those who are struggling and are mourning. At times, we all mourn, but we can prevail through faith, love, prayer, and a positive attitude.

Day 18 — *Be Genuine and Transparent*

One of the things some people struggle with is being straight up and candid with others, to communicate what they truly think and feel. They're afraid of hurting people's feelings and creating conflict.

I wouldn't suggest you spend all your time going around and being opinionated to everyone. That would be sending out a significant negative vibe to the Universe. However, if there is someone important in your life and you have something on your mind, you should respectfully and maturely communicate it. Leaving animated emotion out of the communication allows you to communicate the message clearly.

You cannot control how others will react. If you expressed yourself respectfully, you did the right thing. Now it's up to the other person to return the respect and communicate back. If they don't, you can be at peace that you did the right thing.

There's a mindset we all need to get comfortable with. It's the willingness to have difficult conversations with others. If just the thought of that makes your stomach churn, then this is something you need to develop and improve. Marriages, friendships, parent/children relationships, work situations, partnerships, and team culture would all be more fulfilling if we invested quality time to share our perspectives on the sensitive issues that exist.

This said, there is a healthy process to letting the little things go. Not every friction needs to be discussed. But, the things that weigh on you, continue to frustrate you, that create worries in your mind and spirit, certainly need to be addressed. To be more at peace within yourself, you need to have these important conversations. Keep reminding yourself to have the willingness to have difficult conversations. If the person you need to speak with, whether parent, friend, child, employee, co-worker, client, etc., has a tendency to overreact, start out softly—but start.

Explain to this person that you have something you would like to discuss, that it is out of the love and caring you have for that person that you want to discuss an important topic, that you want to keep the conversation productive where you both have an open mind, and then you have set up the dialog for success.

After that introduction, it's up to you to deliver your thoughts in a respectful, non-accusatory way. While you want to be respectful, don't beat around the bush. Give them a clear understanding of what's on your mind.

Stephen D'Angelo

When they communicate back to you, be open-minded to them. Listen to their perspective, and don't be too quick to talk over them with your views. Truly listen. Be prepared for some candid feedback about your behavior and ways you may be causing them stress. Be open to the feedback just as you want that other person to be open to your perspective.

Then, see if you can come to a mutually acceptable place on this topic. This is especially true in the business world. Too many executives and leaders camouflage their real plans and say what they think will keep their employees going in the direction they want them to go in. This is a culture killer, because employees see the lack of honesty. Then they say what they think their leaders want to hear, and no one is being honest, and they never get to the real issues.

When this happens, sales fall, profits slip, and turnover increases. Then the executives start changing things to solve the problem, and those changes don't deliver the results they want. All this happens while the real issue is genuine transparency and culture. This is the lack of spiritual leadership.

There would be fewer family feuds, angry partners/spouses, deteriorating business relationships, negative company cultures, and festering negative emotions if we all became better at having difficult conversations.

Day 19 — *Have Mental Toughness*

This is one of the keys to success in anything we do in our lives. Parenting, relationships, building a business, being a good student, lasting friendships, a happy career, becoming an actor/actress, training to be a professional athlete— everything requires mental toughness. We all have to deal with adversity, problems, and setbacks. The key question is: how will you mentally deal with this challenge? A mindset of toughness and a desire to overcome the situation in a productive way is the key.

It is understandable to get down once in a while. We all do. You just must make sure you don't stay down. Ask the Universe for help. Really ask with all your heart. Then think through how you will overcome the adversity. Have faith you will succeed. Be determined to overcome the issue. Read a good book for inspiration or seek counseling. Some challenges are very difficult, and we don't need to go at it alone. With mental toughness, you will prevail.

Day 20 — *Strive to Be Humble and Kind*

There is a great country song on this topic that covers it perfectly. It suggests that doing good things in a humble way brings positive energy back to you. When you achieve your goals, reflect on your success, but remain humble. Be sure to appreciate how you got there. You deserve the positive feelings of the achievement.

While you're enjoying your successful feeling, be good to others and help those who are following in your footsteps. Help them get to where they want to go. There is nothing more fulfilling than helping someone achieve their goals. Being humble and kind doesn't mean you are not a fighter, or you don't have grit. I've seen the most competitive people in sports and business fight to win (fairly) but have a heart of gold while appreciating their success and setbacks ... and they stay humble through the process. They then give the same determined effort to help others succeed. People who are humble and kind are very attractive spirits. Many gravitate to them.

Day 21 — *Donate Your Money and Time*

This can be difficult for many people. For some reason, regardless of whether they have an abundance of things/money or very little, they struggle to give some of what they have to others in need. Those who do give some of what they have enjoy the amazing feeling of helping others. This feeling cannot be described. It's a god-like feeling. They are acting as God and helping the world be a better place.

When you give with no expectation of anything in return, great things come back to you. Go and give it a try. Thomas of Villanova, the Spanish friar of the Order of St. Augustine, said it well, "What great profit you gain from God when you are generous! You give a coin and receive a kingdom; you give bread from wheat and receive the Bread of Life; you give a transitory good and receive an everlasting one. You will receive it back, a hundred times more than you offered."

Deliver holiday gifts to children in need, hand food to a homeless person in the street and look them in the eye, or give your time to help someone struggling, and I know you'll feel the great energy of joy in your heart. If all you have is your time, give some of that to a charity. We all make the world a better place when we give back.

Day 22 — *Associate with the People You Want to Be Like*

This can't be stressed enough. We become like the people we associate with … plain and simple. For some people, this is a very difficult thing to follow. Yes, it requires tough decisions, but it's worth it. People cannot give you what they don't have. If they don't have self-discipline, don't live a principled life, don't have much success, struggle financially, or don't display positive energy, then they cannot give those things to you.

Surround yourself with the people who are what you want to be like and have what you want to have. I'm not suggesting you completely disconnect from lifelong friends who no longer share similar goals and a lifestyle that you desire (unless, of course, they are a very negative influence emotionally, psychologically, or mentally, or they abuse drugs, alcohol, etc.). But if you want to achieve certain life goals, be successful, achieve a more positive frame of mind, etc., find people who have achieved this and spend as much time with them as you can. Learn from them. There is no better advice to provide our children. We have seen all-too-often that young adults hang with the wrong crowd and become like that crowd. Birds of a feather flock together

Day 23 — *We All Make Mistakes*

The mistakes we make are our guiding light; that is, if we learn from them and adjust our ways. So many honorable and successful people have shared that they looked at their mistakes squarely in the eye, interpreted them correctly, and then executed behavioral adjustments to allow them to right their course. Fools won't look in the mirror at themselves to see their ill ways and attitudes. Then they wonder why life is always so challenging for them.

Reflect on your mistakes to create an awareness of what went wrong. Don't torture yourself for your missteps, because nothing positive is gained from that. Learn, adjust, and grow. We all come into this world pure, but we become flawed due to the workings and influences of society, but, more importantly, because we are not perfect. We lie, cheat, steal, murder, hurt others' feelings, gossip, bully, mislead, etc.

Some people take a true stock of themselves and their behaviors then make the conscious choice to modify them to stop doing the things that have been holding them back. They make the conscious choice to be different. When they do this, they are amazed at the spiritual newness they experience. This spiritual newness transfers into happiness. These people become happier than they thought they could be.

Another reason why this is important is it helps us to stop judging. When you witness someone committing a wrong, realize you have sinned to, and, rather than condemn or gossip about them, say a silent prayer for them to change their ways. Have empathy. I realize some sins are very hurtful and painful and very hard to forgive, but this is the small gate you have to go through to experience your personal joy. We all mess up from time to time. Face these things and let the guilt go. Then move forward with new behavior.

Day 24 — *Attitude Is Everything*

Ninety-nine percent of the time, your daily attitude determines how your day will turn out. Few things in life will impact the success and happiness of your life than the attitude you bring to it. It is one hundred percent under your control.

Attitude is everything.

When good things happen in your life, are you over the top happy and boastful or internally pleased and thankful. When life's challenges hit you, are you the kind of person who goes down the "this always happens to me" path and panics, or do you take a deep breath, consciously adjust, and put a good attitude to it?

There are endless examples of people who, when faced with adversity, put the right attitude to it and prevailed. There are equally as many who let their negative view of their world put them into a downward spiral. Which are you today and which do you want to become?

Do you want to know what the attitudes of others are? Just look at their natural facial expressions. It's amazing how many people walk around with some sort of scowl on their face, a sad expression, an "I'm beat up" look, or an "I'm jealous face."

Then there are those who radiate love, positive energy, and great possibilities. What does your face say? Don't dismiss this and just assume you have one of those positive and energetic faces. Take an honest inventory of yourself on this. What you sow, so shall you reap. Read inspirational books, watch-uplifting stories, or listen to life-changing speeches, and you will give yourself positive fuel to power a positive attitude.

Attitude is everything.

Your attitude impacts your state of mind. You have the power to control your attitude and state of mind. Things in life happen that make us feel dejected and frustrated, and we can't control these challenging events. What we can control is the state of mind we bring to them. When we hit the challenging times with a constructive and positive attitude, we can change what happens around us. We naturally create a gravitational pull of better things to us. This is the law of cause and effect. Have a positive and uplifting attitude and you will attract great things.

Attitude is everything.

Day 25 — *Work on Being Healthy*

What do you eat every day? Do you exercise during the week? Are you a picture of health or not so much? Be honest with yourself. If you had to pick one, healthy or unhealthy, which would it be?

Other than having a personal relationship with God, taking care of yourself is the most important thing you can do. Obesity rates in the United States continue to rise higher and higher each year. We eat too many packaged and processed foods, and we eat way too much quantity of foods on a daily basis, such as refined sugars, starchy carbs, etc.

While it is more expensive to eat healthily, you don't have to break the bank to do this. Just change some habits. Eat more raw and cooked vegetables, eat more fish, be moderate with beef, etc. There are so many great books available on healthy eating for you to read and implement.

Often, people can't admit their diet is less than average. To that, I suggest they write down every morsel of food they eat for one day. Every tea, every spoon of sugar they put in their coffee, every piece of candy, every potato chip, every vegetable ... everything. At around 9 p.m., look at the list you created and grade yourself. If you let your body become overweight, you are most likely planning a shorter life.

167

Day 26 — *Have Balance*

Many of us get so excited about our new project, new job, new opportunity, or new passion that we lose balance. Relationships suffer, our energy suffers, and our health suffers, because we are too "all in" on this one thing. To achieve anything great takes a lot of effort and focus and, unless you put the right amount of positive work into it, you won't succeed.

So, do a personal check-up. Are you coming up for a breather once in a while? Are you going to dinner with your spouse/partner and leaving the smart phone home so you can concentrate on your relationship? Are you committing to spending time with your children? Are you going for a run a few times a week?

The point is, being great at anything requires commitment, but we must monitor our actions so that we don't ruin our relationships and our health in the process. Set your goals, work hard to achieve them, grind, give it your all, BUT find time each day to take a breather and find days where you can recharge your batteries by relaxing, walking the beach, sitting quietly, or doing whatever gives you peace of mind, body, and spirit.

Day 27 — *We All Need Mentors*

This principle goes two ways. One way is for you to accept mentorship, and the other way is for you to give it. Let's start with you receiving mentorship, coaching, and guidance.

The fastest way for you to get from where you are to where you want to be is to seek out the people who have already done what you want to do and ask them if they will help you achieve the same goal. They did what you want to do, they got hit with the setbacks and adversity, and they found ways around the obstacles ... and prevailed! And, guess what, 99.99% of the people will be happy to help and tell you what they did.

Some people refuse to ask for help. This is foolish, egocentric, and reveals insecurity. If you are one of the people who think you're too big to ask for help (ego), afraid to ask (insecurity), or you just don't think it will help (foolishness), I plead with you to deal with the pain of changing yourself and go find a mentor. You will achieve your goal in half the time if you have a mentor guiding you.

Even the most successful people look to others for assistance when they have big decisions to make. They leverage their network or go to the two or three people they completely trust for guidance.

The second part of mentorship is to give it. I have already written about doing good things for others, and this is one of the greatest things you can do. If someone comes to you and asks for help, give it. If you are really good at something and you see someone you know who is struggling, offer your expertise. Mentoring/coaching others and then witnessing them achieving their goal is very satisfying. Doing this also brings the right spiritual energy back to you and impacts your life in a positive way.

Day 28 — *Seek Wisdom*

One of the critical things that will impact where you are one year from today is how much wisdom of others you tap into. One great way to seek wisdom is to read great books. When I say "books," in today's technological world with our access to so much content, I mean paper books, audio books, YouTube videos, reading content on the Internet, etc. The point is that you will accelerate your positive progress in this life by reading books, accessing content, listening to podcasts and watching videos published by people who have already done what you want to do.

Maybe your goal is a more healthy weight, to be happier, to improve your health, to be the greatest dentist in the world, a better parent, a better student, a more impactful spiritual leader, a better communicator, achieve greater goals, be a champion athlete, be a more effective leader ... it doesn't matter what you want, other people have experienced what you want and they have written books about it.

If you want to change your world, read a new book every month and your conscious and subconscious mind will be transformed into a machine that attracts what you want. While you look for the books that will help you, include the greatest book of all time ... the Bible.

If you want to be happy, successful, and transform your life, spend time reading the Bible just a little each day. The lessons Jesus shared in the New Testament apply today. Candidly, it doesn't matter if you believe that Jesus is the son of God or not, the lessons are ageless and valid. If you read his teachings and think deeply about them, you will receive divine guidance in most aspects of your life. The key is to think deeply about them after you read them. Ask yourself, "What does this mean to me?" or "How can I apply this in my life?" Doing so contributes to a new you and your single day of peace. I promise.

Day 29 — *Make Good Decisions*

Where we are today is a result of the decisions we made and actions we have taken leading up to today. If you want your life situation to change, evaluate your decisions and actions and change. Take one hundred percent of the accountability for yourself and where you are today. You are the master of your own fate. Every decision you make steers your life in a direction. Inside of you is your inner voice that guides you. Listen to it. It is your spirit and your soul guiding you.

At times, we are all a victim of things happening to us beyond our control. There's no question about that. But, even when life throws you a curve ball, if you make it a habit that you consciously evaluate your attitude and subsequent decisions which lead to the actions you take, you will clearly see when you are defeating yourself or positively enabling yourself.

If you want better relationships, look at the decisions you've made to attract the people in your life. If you want different people in your life, make different decisions. If you want to be a better student, look at your decisions and how you can change them. If you want more money, evaluate your spending and saving decisions. If you want to be a better parent, evaluate how you have led your children and make changes. If you want to be sober, take responsibility for your drinking decisions. It is never too late to make better decisions.

If you evaluate your good and regrettable decisions, the ones that came from your gut and your intuition are probably the ones that turned out to be the best. Those are the ones when you let God speak to you and you followed the divine guidance. That inner voice is God, because God is in you.

The more you ignore your inner voice and make decisions based on peer pressure, what other people will think, what other people want, the more challenging your life will be. The more you listen to your inner self, the better your decisions and life will be.

Your purpose in life is to live and be the best you, the most fulfilled you. Listening to your inner voice gets you there. Hope is not a strategy. You cannot live your life hoping things will turn out the way you want them to. You have to take the responsibility to make the decisions that move your life in the direction you want. That being said, the best thing we can do is to teach our youth this principle. The sooner they can take complete control of this philosophy and consciously make better decisions—listen to their spirit and soul more—they will be put on the path to life happiness and success.

Day 30 – *Persistence*

Acquiring persistence will allow you to move forward faster in this world. Few things can replace persistence to achieve the goals you set. If there is something you want, something you believe in, something you are passionate about, then you should be willing to persist to achieve the objective you want.

We all heard the stories about writers who got turned down by thirty or forty publishers only to get one that said yes. That "yes" changed their lives. Or the hugely successful actor/actress who got turned down for movie roles over and over but, through their persistence, they got the perfect role for themselves and it catapulted them to great success. There is story after story of people who achieved great things by just not giving up.

Thomas Edison failed hundreds of times when he tried to get a light bulb to stay lit. He said that he never failed, he just learned many ways it wouldn't work. That is the right attitude. Every rejection gets you closer to an acceptance. The law of averages is a universal law and, if you use it in your favor, you will succeed. You will realize that every time you don't succeed, it brings you closer to success.

The truth is that the prizes we want hardly ever come in the beginning. They come near the end of hard work and persistence. If you quit too soon, you'll never realize your goal. If you're not a naturally persistent person, use the principle of self-suggestions to become more persistent. To achieve great things, it boils down to a daily focus on your goal, concentrating on it, remaining committed and determined to achieve it, and having the self-discipline to do what is required to succeed. Persistence results in success.

Day 31 — *Be Thankful*

Not many things will create deep inner happiness and attract great things into your life as much as demonstrating gratitude—gratitude for everything in your life, the good and the not so good. If you take the attitude that all the things going on in your life are there for a positive purpose and thank God and His/Her almighty power for bringing this into your life, you will get through the bad times more easily and bring more good things into your life.

Everyone on this planet has something they can be thankful for. Most of us have many, MANY things to be thankful for. The problem is that we don't take the time to recognize and acknowledge these things. We take them for granted. We don't mean to, but we're so busy chasing the day that we don't stop to be thankful for our health, the job we have, the friends we have, where we live, the sun, the rain, that we have a home ... everything.

Every morning think of three things you want to be thankful for that day. Then, try to think gratitude thoughts about those three things during the day. The art of gratitude has an amazing spiritual effect. God has given us the opportunity to have a wonderful life. Gratitude is what starts and keeps the wonderful life coming. Be thankful.

Day 32— *Meditate*

Meditation has become very popular over the last few years. This is a great thing, because meditation transforms lives. Nothing has had more of a positive impact on my life than the activity of meditation. Even during my most challenging times, I would get into a relaxing meditative state and visualize what I wanted to be and have in my life versus what my experiences were at that time. This attracted those things to me, and I eventually received them. Maybe what arrived wasn't exactly as I pictured in my mind, but when they arrived, they were perfect. The higher power of universal energy brought me these things in the way I needed them.

There are beliefs that Jesus not only meditated, but he taught his disciples that they should also meditate. Further beliefs are that when Jesus spent all those days in the desert, he spent time meditating and listening to God. Jesus taught his followers (Mark 11:24) "Therefore I say unto you, what things so ever ye desire, when ye pray, believe that ye receive them, and ye shall have them."

When we pray to God and His/Her universal power, Jesus taught us to visualize that we see ourselves already being granted the prayer, which is a key part of meditation. Jesus also said, "But seek first the kingdom of God and all its righteousness, and these things shall be given to you." (Matthew 6:33)

I believe one part of the interpretation of the "kingdom" he referred to is the kingdom inside all of us—that kingdom of God that we have inside of us that we can tap into. Meditation taps into that kingdom. Meditation will calm you, help you think more clearly, heal you, bring to you the things you want in this world, and get you more in touch with the positive energy of this world. There are many methods and variations of meditation. Do the research and find one that resonates with you and practice it.

Day 33 — *Take the Risk of Loving Someone*

Opening up our hearts to love someone makes us vulnerable. This can be extremely scary. Many don't want to take that risk, because they fear the possibility of pain and heartbreak. For them, the possible pain is a greater de-motivator than the motivator of the possible joy they might feel by experiencing love.

It is a very interesting human dynamic that we are more motivated to avoid pain than to gain pleasure. If you dissect human behavior, you will see that the actions of most are much more driven to avoid pain. Because of this, we take too few risks in our lives.

The one I'm covering here is the risk of the loss of love. The wonderful fulfillment of having love in your life cannot be compared with anything else. The Bible says, "And now these three remain: faith, hope and love. But the greatest of these is love."

When we think of this topic, we automatically think of romantic love, a partner in our lives. But this also applies to friendships. While we're on this Earth, we will have the opportunity to have some real genuine friendships. The non-judgmental love and generosity we give to these friendships creates a fulfilled life. We all need friends ... loyal friends. Then comes our neighbors. Jesus taught us to love our neighbors as ourselves. Basically, it means we should be pleasant and loving to all. It comes back in spades if we do that.

So, the risk is, we give love and don't get it back in return. If we don't, we have the peace of mind to know we tried. I promise, if you keep giving the love, you WILL get plenty back in return. Today, tell your partner, friend, family member you love them.

Day 34 - *Connect Better with Others*

We all know the saying "It takes a village ...." We use that phrase when we want to explain that we cannot do some things on our own. Often, the most significant things we want to accomplish require more than just our individual effort ... raising a family, building a new school, helping the poor, building a business, mentoring teenagers, advancing your career, etc. We need the effort and positive spirit of others to get the job done properly.

The responsibility we have is to effectively emotionally connect with the people we need and want to work with us. This idea of connecting is very important for everyone to be consciously aware of. Connecting effectively starts with eye contact. If you really want to connect with someone, you have to look them in the eye with genuine interest, almost to the point where you're projecting love to that person.

I'm not talking about a brief look in someone's eyes and then shifting your focus elsewhere. I'm talking about a sincere, lengthy eye connection. This sounds very obvious but try monitoring how you make eye connections with others. Monitor how others make eye contact with you. Most people connect the eyes for a few brief seconds, and then they drift their eyes to all sorts of different places. Monitor this and you will recognize this tendency in yourself and those you associate with.

Also important in connecting with others is to be very aware of the energy you are projecting to the world. Are you always absorbed with the challenges of your life and projecting negative and "edgy" energy? Are you always talking about yourself and what is going on in your family, business, and social circles? In other words, are you self-absorbed? Or, are you genuinely interested in others and making the conscious decision to be a source of positive energy that is genuinely curious of other people, regardless of what is going on in your life? If you want to bring the right people into your life who will help you advance in the areas where you want to progress, give off positive energy and genuinely connect with others through your sincere eye contact and interest in them.

Day 35 - *Be Silent*

The phrase "silence is golden" has merit. We live in a world where we are bombarded with marketing messages, emails, negative news stations, text messages, pop up advertisements, opinions of others, radio talk shows, etc. It is truly overwhelming.

Did you know that the average person is exposed to 4,000 to 10,000 advertisements a day? When you add in all the other conversations, distractions, and public noise, the number is astronomical.

With all of these distractions, how can you tap into your inner self and the wisdom of the universal energy of God? It is very healthy to disconnect from all the "noise" for a few minutes a day and just be silent. With silence, your conscious and subconscious minds have the chance to speak to you. God has a chance to whisper things into your ear.

When you are quiet for a period of time, the universal intelligence comes to you. You'll be amazed with the wonderful, clarifying thoughts you'll have when you sit in silence for a while. When driving, shut off the radio and cell phone once in a while. Drive in silence and think. What are your thoughts? Evaluate them. Are they positive in tone or negative? Think about your goals. What problems do you want to solve? What important decisions do you have to make? What good do you want to give to this world?

Go somewhere and be silent. Close your eyes and take a few deep breaths to relax. Just be still and think. The universal intelligence will whisper thoughts to you. Silence is a form of meditation. Many very successful people start their day with thirty minutes of silence. They go to a private room and disconnect from everything. They have a pad and pen at their desk and, in their solitude, thoughts come to mind, and they write them down. They reveal that the solutions to their most pressing problems come to them, their greatest product ideas come to them, and their most inspiring ideas come to them. Silence is divine.

Day 36 - *Have Empathy*

Putting yourself in someone else's shoes and understanding their perspective and situation opens the door to productive and loving collaboration. Human nature is to judge, to see what is going on with a person, and to have all the answers. Those people who think they have all the answers are limiting themselves. They put themselves in a box of their own self-righteous views. They can be about inter-racial relationships, bi-sexual situations, problems someone is causing in their own life, career challenges, family challenges, or friendship challenges.

The art of empathy is to listen and try to feel what the other person is feeling. You may have some good advice for that person, but the advice you give will be emotionally ignored until the other person feels you understand them. This saying by Stephen Covey hits the mark perfectly, "Seek first to understand and then to be understood."

In the Bible, Jesus said "Why do you look at the speck of sawdust in your brother's eye and pay no attention to the plank in your own eye?" Think about that. How many times do we see things wrong with others, yet we don't see even greater things wrong with ourselves, things that we should spend time correcting? Having empathy allows us to not focus on and criticize the speck of dust but on what it must feel like to have it.

Day 37 – *Lean Not on Your Own Understanding*

As you partake in this journey of transforming yourself, you will come upon times when things seem as if they're going in the wrong direction. It will seem like nothing is going right for you and that all this positive energy creation, goal setting, and positive expectancy may be a waste of time.

I tell you this: lean not on your own understanding. What this means is that we humans think we have it all figured out, and exactly how we should get from where we are to where we want to be. But God and the universal power of God know better. The universal energy knows the exact things that have to happen to get you to where you want to be.

Maybe you just lost your job, and you think that this is a huge setback. But, maybe the Universe knows better and got you out of that job to get you into a better one, one that will get you to the goals you set. It could be you or your child didn't get accepted in his/her desired university, or maybe you became ill, and you feel this is a huge downer. Have faith that God and the universal power is guiding you to your ultimate desired destination. It just may not be the path you think it should be.

The university your child gets into could be where she/he makes all the right contacts for the career they want, or they meet the love of their life! The point here is, when things don't go as you want them and you feel frustration, lean not on your own understanding but on God's. Tell God you have full faith in Him/Her and Her/His energy even if you don't quite understand it right now. Surrender while you execute all these daily principles. It's a bit of a dichotomy where you must set your goals, visualize that you have achieved what you want to achieve, be a source of positive energy, work hard, etc... but our understanding isn't the ultimate genius. If you have faith and you keep a positive frame of mind while you have challenges and you follow these principles, you will prevail.

Day 38 – *Save for a Secure Life*

This principle may appear to be very obvious and academic. While very basic in theory, this is where millions of people falter. As obvious and fundamental as this concept is, pay close attention to these words and adhere. If you do, it will guide you to a secure financial future. If you don't, your life will be burdened with the frustration of feeling you are constantly running a losing race.

Finances are an important part of our life. Many people, marriages, families, friendships, businesses, and religious institutions have crumbled due to the stress of finances. Overspending, over borrowing, living beyond your means, trying to keep up with the Joneses, and poor investments driven by greed and ego are just some of the culprits to financial challenges and, ultimately, ruin.

How many times have you heard stories of very wealthy athletes, musicians, lottery winners, and successful businesspeople losing it all after having accumulated tens and hundreds of millions of dollars? Unfortunately, it happens all too often. This is caused by overspending and not managing your money (and ego) properly.

If you want to be financially secure, keep your spending in check. Put yourself on a budget and do not waiver. As you make more money, stay on this budget. Live within your means. Better yet, live lower than your means. You may be thinking: how can I accumulate the money I need to be financially independent? The answer to that is to save a percentage of every dollar you make. It is the easiest and hardest thing to do. Before you pay any bill, pay yourself first!

Here's the secret. If every time you get a paycheck, receive money as a gift, are paid for the services you provide, etc., save a minimum of ten percent (the higher percentage you save, the faster you become independently wealthy) of the gross payment before taxes and any of the standard payroll deductions. So, if you just made $1,000, save at least $100.

This may sound like an amount that won't make any difference in your life, but it does. The habit of saving this money and putting it into your investment account will be set in stone for when you receive larger amounts of money. This habit will make you independently wealthy. I define independently wealthy as the monthly income you receive from your investments exceeds your monthly expenses.

That means, if you don't work, you can still live as you are and the return on your investments covers all your living costs. How does this happen? Through saving and the power of compound interest. If you don't know how compound interest works, look it up on the Internet, and you'll learn about this immense power.

As you accumulate money in your investment account and you see it grow through the power of compound interest, you will be tested. You'll want to take some of that money and buy a new car or some material item that is a depreciating asset (the value goes down over time). Resist this temptation.

This money is only to be used for asset appreciation items ... investments. If you use some of this money for material gain, you are shutting off the supply of your growing wealth. If you want some material items, use the money after you have paid yourself first (the 10% minimum).

Anyone at any income level can achieve financial independence (per my definition) by following this guidance. You don't have to be making a significant income. For those who know of this principle but are not living it, you must ask yourself why. Don't be like the sad individual who many years later regrets their lack of saving discipline. Save your money and invest it wisely.

Day 39 – *Satisfaction Over More Things*

How about getting a new car, the newest fad in sneakers, a $6,000 handbag, another vacation, a diamond ring, a Cartier watch, another home, a bigger home, a beach home, a boat, a bigger boat, a Cartier bracelet, a Maserati, more shoes, a custom suit, a new pool, waterfalls for the pool, or a Mercedes for the kids? While there is nothing wrong with acquiring material things, the number of things we want is endless. Acquiring things is often fulfilling because it is the signal that the hard work we put in delivered an improvement in our life. We achieved a goal. The things we visualized and committed to did arrive.

This is great. However, the warning is that many people connect their self-worth with getting more material things. This is very dangerous. This is the syndrome that there is never enough. Things do not make our lives happy. If there are things going wrong in your life and you're not feeling completely happy inside, the accumulation of cars, jewelry, clothes etc. will not fix this.

Address the issues you're dealing with head on. Doing so will get them resolved. Then, you'll feel the joy of the things your hard work brought to you. Things make us feel good if they are balanced with conscious satisfaction and gratitude. Did you get that new watch for the right reasons? Did you feel satisfied with the things you had before you got the new watch?

This is the critical thing. We must look at what we already have with gratitude and satisfaction, so we are grounded in peace. If we genuinely appreciate what we have and know what we have is really enough … we really don't need anything more … then additional material things will come with a healthy mindset and balanced emotions.

You know if you're off track if, as you acquire things, they aren't enough, and you need the next thing to make you happy. Or, someone you know got something new, and you feel down about it. This is a very unhealthy way to go through life. We all want new and nice things. All good. Like I stated, as long as you aren't under the influence of "things bring me happiness."

Jesus said, "It's easier for a camel to go through the eye of a needle than for a rich man to enter the kingdom of heaven." What did he mean? Did he intend to be literal? Did he refer to the heaven we think about going to when we die? What I think he meant by this teaching is that those who are financially rich can get so caught up in becoming richer and having more things, that it becomes a burden. And, the Kingdom of Heaven he refers to can be the joy and happiness that is here on Earth. If we are constantly dissatis-fied, how can we enjoy this wonderful world we live in? Count your blessings today.

Day 40 – *Listen*

This is about communication skills and being better connected to the people around us. Probably the most loving and caring thing we can do for someone is to listen to him or her and investing our time to listen with the intent to understand. When we think about communication, we often think about how we speak and what we say. Those who have the best communication skills listen the best. They listen to understand. They don't constantly interrupt others.

The Dalai Lama said it best, "When you talk, you are only repeating what you already know. But, if you listen, you may learn something new." When it's time for great communicators to talk, they do so in a satisfying pace with enthusiasm. But, first and foremost, they listen.

Listen to your children … how many children give the signal that parents are annoying because they constantly preach? Listen to your spouse, your friend, your partner, you employees, your customers, your congregation, and your boss. If you listen and digest, even if you disagree with what you're hearing, you will have a more productive engagement and more personal satisfaction.

Too many people are too busy talking, and they don't hear anything. Take a breath and listen. When you do, people feel you care. When they feel you care, they trust you more. When they trust you more, they become closer to you, and together you can have a more fulfilling relationship. Learn the art of listening.

Day 41 – *Forgiveness*

One of the most negative energies we can have through our bodies and spirit is anger, resentment, and downright hatred for others. The negative feelings you have for someone else don't hurt that person—they hurt you. We have all been hurt. Parents let us down, friends betray us, a spouse cheats, a sibling lies ... and, worse, a loved one could be killed.

All these hurtful things allow us to justify our anger towards people and God. We believe we have the right to wish ill will on others because of the harm they caused us. The ability to let go of grudges and wanting revenge is very difficult but doing so sets you on a new free course in your life. Never forget, the law of negative energy is such that it only comes back to you. Without you knowing it, you are making your life worse by not forgiving. Maybe at a fraction of an inch at a time but, in time, all those fractions of inches add up to miles.

Forgiving others brings positive energy to you. Yes, it can be very hard to do because of the pain and problems you endured. But your burden of anger will disappear once you truly forgive them and ask the higher power to do the same. By forgiving, you are not feeling that what had been done to you is acceptable, and you are not welcoming the person who did you harm.

You can still be frustrated and sad over the pain others have caused you but, if you genuinely tell God and the Universe that you forgive this person and wish no ill will on them, and you ask God and the Universe to do the same, you become free.

This also goes for forgiving yourself. We have all done things we regret. Maybe you made decisions that created a detrimental situation to yourself or others. Forgive yourself. Pray to God and confess your mistakes and ask for forgiveness. If you do it genuinely, you are forgiven. Recognize the error you made and make today and tomorrow better. Start new.

Jesus displayed the ultimate forgiveness while on the cross, and he asked his Father in heaven to forgive those who persecuted him because "they know not what they do." Forgiveness cleanses your inner being, sets you free, and returns happiness into your life. Forgiveness leaves the past in the past and moves you forward. Forgiveness gives you a new life. Forgiveness sets you free to new positive things. Who can you forgive today?

Day 42 – *Laugh at Yourself*

Sometimes we all take ourselves too seriously. While life is serious and we need to be focused and disciplined to achieve the goals we set, we also need the balance of a lite heart.

A lite heart allows us to laugh at ourselves. We all experience blunders and while we naturally try to cover up and overcome them, if we laugh at ourselves, we progress forward more quickly.

Think about some of the mistakes you have made. Aren't some of them comical? Haven't you told stories about your blunders? We laugh and tell people stories of how we totally messed things up. We laugh at our silly mistakes. The secret is to laugh sooner!

It may seem odd but we may be happiest when we laugh at our past mishaps and turn them into entertainment for others. What if I told you that laughing at yourself can actually make you healthier? It is true, science has said that it relaxes our nerves and can improve our health.

Science also tells us that when we poke fun at ourselves, we exhibit greater levels of emotional well-being. We appear more self-confident and are more attractive to others when we can tell a funny story about ourselves. Those that can laugh at her/himself reflect a higher degree of self-worth, and that is an attractive attribute.

Laughter releases dopamine, increases blood flow, strengthens the heart and leads to increased optimism. That enables us to thrive when we are faced with challenges and adversity.

Go ahead, tell funny stories about yourself and laugh. When things go wrong, try to laugh sooner.

Day 43 – *Discipline Yourself*

Self-discipline is critical to a successful life. This sets you apart from ninety-five percent of everyone else on this Earth. The sad truth is that most people don't have self-discipline, and they wonder why they always take one step forward and two steps back. It could be their career, their diet, their exercise plan, achieving goals they think they desire, accumulating financial assets, etc.

Watch the most successful people you know. They are disciplined, almost mechanical in focus. They have a plan for each day and, for the most part, they don't waver from it. They don't let the whims and emotions that hit them alter their planned actions. Don't be fooled; they get whims and emotional distractions just like everyone else, but what makes them different is that they are stronger inside. They feel the emotional distraction, recognize what it is, and command themselves to stay on their plan and the course they set. They assess how they are doing and, if changes are needed, they make them. That is self-discipline.

While they find time for "chilling out" and "down time," most of their day is focused on doing the most important thing moment by moment that is in sync with their goals and plans. They are productive at doing the most important thing most of the time.

You can be productive too. It's a decision you have to make and utilize the right self-talk/self-programing to continue on the proper path. When you do this moment by moment throughout the day, by the end of the year you see you have become a dramatically different person. Your actions are in line with your goals and not your sporadic thoughts, distractions, and emotions. You transform into a much better and happier you.

Day 44 – *Spiritual Leadership*

We can all be spiritual leaders. All walks of life should lead people with the proper principles. This concept is something more businesspeople need to embrace. If you're not a businessperson, you still need to be a spiritual leader to have a happy life and be a positive force in our world.

What is a spiritual leader? A spiritual leader is someone who balances a blend of attributes. They hold people accountable, they help people with continuous improvement to inspire growth, they are committed to winning, they are empathetic, they genuinely care about their people, they are transparent so people trust them, they listen very well, they are willing to have the difficult conversations in a productive way, they respect diversity and different opinions, they allow others to be themselves, they constantly monitor their progress, they create an environment of fun, they have a process they follow, and they are very disciplined.

How would you like to work for someone like this? Most people love working in this environment, because they grow, and they feel they're a bigger part of the mission. If you're a parent, what if you displayed these attributes with your children? How much happier and more successful would they be? What if you're a spiritual leader? How much more fulfilled would your congregation be? What if you're a husband/wife/partner? How much more engaged and happier would your partner be with you?

Spiritual leadership dramatically improves the performance and satisfaction of those you lead—employees, children, etc. It's the new way to create a culture where everyone wins.

The opposite of this tears down love and performance. Think about the parent who doesn't genuinely listen to their children's ideas or beliefs and is always telling them what the child should or shouldn't do. Make no mistake about it, the child is tuning you out emotionally.

What if you're a business leader that only cares about the company performance and doesn't deeply understand the human aspect these principles provide? Regardless of the success you may be having, you are not reaching your potential. The trust of family members, children, employees, life partners, and business partners is built in drops and lost in buckets. Execute these spiritual leadership attributes and you will build a bucket of trust, love, and great performance. How can you be more of a spiritual leader today?

Day 45 – *Be Your Best and Keep Making Your Best Better*

Focusing on growth is a very healthy way to live. We are either getting better or worse. We never stay the same. If you want to be continually inspired, motivated, energized, feel valuable, be your best, then continuously improve yourself.

Continuous learning is the ongoing process of improving your knowledge and capabilities of what you do for a living, or the process of learning new things that inspire you. Focus on what is important to you and write down the things you want to improve.

Do you want to be a better parent, friend, partner, athlete, salesperson, teacher, or whatever is important to you? Just get a little better every day, and you'll have a more fulfilled life. As you do this, you'll enjoy the wonder of personal growth.

Do doctors graduate from medical school and then never learn anything new about their chosen medical field? Of course not. They are required to engage in continuous education so that they understand human conditions more completely, as well as the new technical advancements available to help their patients. Thank God they do!

We should view our own profession the same way. Are you a physical therapist? If so, read newly published material and take the courses that keep you on the cutting edge of your trade. Are you a horticulturist? If so, learn about all the new advancements in caring for gardens of all kinds.

Are you a sales professional? Then learn all the new approaches to understanding your prospect's needs and presenting solutions that bring value to your market. Are you a stay-at-home parent? Then learn how to be a more patient, loving, and supportive parent.

There are a ton of free resources on the Internet to give you guidance on how you can improve in the areas that are important to you. Learn from them and then take action. Grow and feel the amazing self-satisfaction of becoming a better and stronger person. People who don't aspire to grow are often crabby and irritable. Continuously learn and keep moving forward.

Day 46 – *Control Your Emotions*

Few things have hurt careers, marriages, friendships, or parent/children relationships and overall happiness more than losing control of our emotions and saying and doing things we regret. We all get angry and feel anxiety. We all want to give people a piece of our mind. We all get tired of always having to deal with other people's insensitivities, their lies, and their baggage. At times, we all just want to let loose on them.

The short-term pleasure of unloading verbally on others is not worth the long-term pain you'll feel by damaging the relationship--damage that may be beyond repair. It is much healthier to take a few deep breaths, stay calm, and articulate your position calmly.

If the situation is too tense, then get out of the environment you're in and return at a later date to discuss things. The high road is the better road. To better understand your desire to retaliate, look at the ego. The ego inside of us wants us to be right, be first, be better, show others what we are, or show others we are smart, strong, and special. The ego is what tells you to attack the person who is getting on your last nerve.

We can learn something from Buddhism if we want to reduce ego's drive within ourselves. Buddhism teaches us to let go of the ego by never being better than anyone else. There is no need for physical things. Just be in a constant state of contentment and pleasure.

Great athletes who perform flawlessly under pressure have found a way to control their emotions. Surgeons executing very delicate surgeries do so smoothly by controlling their emotions, and the parents who help their children "off the ledge" when they're dealing with a significant problem keep their emotions in check to create calm.

If you have difficulty controlling your emotions, get help from a professional or find a great book on this topic. Improve. Something will happen today that will get your emotions going in a non-productive way. How will you stay emotionally balanced and be productive?

Day 47 – *Get Your Sleep*

There have been numerous studies and books written about the power of sleep. I suggest you get one and read it. Research has revealed the correlation of seven or more hours of sleep per night and a healthier and happier person. Sleep less than that and you could be increasing your chances of getting cancer, dementia, and other very serious diseases.

The amount of sleep you get each night impacts your emotional state, weight, diet, ability to fight off sickness, ability to communicate, your grades in school, creativity, and the ability to perform in your chosen field. As a matter of fact, studies have shown that surgeons who have six or fewer hours of sleep per night make the most mistakes during surgery.

The research on the power of sleep is immense, and I suggest you tap into it and learn. The younger generation has the tendency to remain awake until deep into the night. Access to their smart phone, technology, and so much streaming content keeps them entertained hour after hour. If you add in social media, it's a recipe for lack of good quality sleep ... night after night. These sleep habits eventually catch up to us and hinder our ability to function at a high level. Moodiness, irritable behavior, and poor life performance is the result. What changes can you make in your lifestyle that will give you a healthy seven or more hours of sleep per night?

Day 48 - *You Don't Have to Start Out as #1*

Too often, people get discouraged because they don't start out being the first or the best—the first one hired, the first one promoted, the first in their class, on the starting team, or the first in the draft of life. The amazing positive thing about the universal energy of this world is that no one is so far behind that they can't catch up and achieve the success they want, and no one is too far ahead that others can't catch up to them.

With faith, commitment, and hard work, all things are possible. You don't have to start out in the #1 position to be successful. If anything demonstrates this point, it's that of the famous NFL quarterback Tom Brady. Out of college, he had to wait until the 166th draft pick. While it is always impressive to be drafted to a professional sports team, the 166th pick certainly doesn't have the ring of "the first round."

However, Tom Brady went on to become if not the greatest then one of the greatest quarterbacks of all time. He didn't let not being number one deter him. Don't let it deter you. It doesn't matter where you start out. What matters is to get in the game (whatever your game is) and put in the hard work with a positive attitude and become great.

Follow and execute the principles you are reading here, and you'll prevail. History is full of stories about people who started from measly beginnings but built great things. For example, I know a group of parents that started a school for children with autism in the basement of a church with one student and, in time, built a specialized educational institution of over thirty autistic children.

A person with only $10 in his pocket could start his own business and build an empire. How about the walk-on athlete who didn't get any scholarships but became the best player in the division? It doesn't matter where you start. What matters is where you end. Make the time between your beginning and ending great. If you do, you will experience your success.

Day 49 – *Be a Great Coach*

Just as one-on-one coaching is a critical aspect for effective leaders in business, coaching the people in your life demonstrates spiritual leadership, because you help them grow. Great coaching is not telling, demanding, or preaching. While there are times when direct, firm communication is required, most coaching is done best when you listen attentively to someone's situation and then communicate specifics to help them.

Great coaching is when you recognize when someone has performed great as well as when improvements and adjustments are needed. Great coaching is also displaying "tough love" and delivering a difficult message that someone needs to hear.

Productive coaching is also the secret to effective parenting when children reach those early teenage years and begin to become independent thinkers. They care less about what their mom and dad preach. They want to be heard and, if they are, they'll be open to coaching.

Great coaches get the most from their friends, team, employees, and children, because they put so much into them. Can you recall someone who has been a great coach to you in sports, business, or life? If you have had the blessing of a great coach, you'll probably recall several things about them. They probably knew their field expertly well, displayed excellent listening skills, exercised transparency, provided authentic praise and reprimands when appropriate, challenged you, held you accountable, had an energy about them you became attracted to, had a fun spirit to be around, and truly wanted to win.

Be like that person you remember. Who in your life needs coaching? Who needs someone who will listen to their situation and then provide effective and meaningful coaching suggestions to help them get from where they are to where they want to be? Find that person and be a genuine coach.

Day 50 – *The Final Daily Principle – Enthusiasm*

While the final principle is enthusiasm, it is by no means the least important. Quite the contrary. Enthusiasm is a special power we all have and must use if we expect to attract great things to our lives. It is a requirement if we are going to inspire those around us.

With enthusiasm and faith, we can achieve great things. Enthusiasm is contagious and, when you approach people with the energy of enthusiasm, you display confidence, and people will gravitate to you. When you attack your goals with enthusiasm, you create the attracting energy to make them become a reality.

When you are enthusiastic, you tell the world you believe in yourself, you are going places, and you are a positive person who offers "can do" energy. I'm not talking about over-the-top enthusiasm that can be perceived as fake and manufactured. I'm referring to a calm and positive enthusiastic energy in everything you do—an energy that has a smile on your face, a look of happiness in your eyes, and confidence with an attitude that you are excited with life.

How many people do you encounter on a daily basis who lack enthusiasm? You see and feel it immediately just by looking at them. They don't have to say a word, and you can feel if they are positive and enthusiastic. Attract the people and events you want in your life by doing everything with enthusiasm, even the mundane things you must do. Put positive enthusiasm into them and they will be less mundane.

If you're like some people who have a difficult time being enthusiastic because they just don't feel it, I say to be enthusiastic, act enthusiastic. If you force yourself to act enthusiastic in a very conscious way, you will find that you become more and more naturally enthusiastic. You transform into the person who energizes everything around you with enthusiasm. If you want people to accept your ideas, agree with your perspective, fund your business, learn from you, purchase your products or services, agree to have a date with you, hire you, or promote you, then use the power of enthusiasm to make it happen. To be enthusiastic, act enthusiastic.

CONCLUSION

Two Years Later

Over the last twenty-four months, Father Mark Tossi has traveled throughout North America, Europe, the U.K., the Nordic Countries, and Asia sharing his philosophies on spiritual leadership and living a happy, healthy, and more fruitful life. He has worked with religious leaders, business executives, corporations, and educational institutions, all with the intent to help them be more successful and happier with their lives. He has been teaching people how to achieve a single day of peace, one day at a time, and he has appeared on various news programs and talk shows spreading his philosophies.

With the publishing of his book, his popularity increased throughout many religious societies. He has been invited to share his spirituality in various religious ceremonies including Jewish synagogues and temples, in Presbyterian, Lutheran, and Catholic churches. He enjoyed experiences in Hindu and Buddhist temples as well as Muslim Mosques.

While he continued to be a practicing Catholic, he consciously opened his spiritual awareness to many religions in order to learn and grow. His motivation is to share with all religious participants that no religion is superior, and they all have valuable teachings. It is up to each of us to select the religion that speaks most clearly to our spirit, and we shall not pass judgment on others ... as long as their main principle is based on love and peace for all. At each of the religious ceremonies he participated in, he continued to deliver his inspiring vision as to how all religions need to adjust and change to better serve the world.

Father Mark and Jonathan Crew continue their correspondence via email and phone calls. When Father Mark is in the New Jersey or New York area, he frequently meets with Jonathan. Jonathan often reminds Father Mark how well his book, *A Single Day of Peace*, is selling and encourages him to think about a second book. Father Mark often reminds Jonathan to do honorable things with his share of the proceeds. Jonathan acknowledges this and advises he gives generously to charitable activities.

What is next for Father Mark? He doesn't know. He's taking things one day at a time, as he shares his positive inspiration creating a single day of peace for others.

This is not "The End" but another new beginning.

MESSAGE FROM THE AUTHOR

I hope you found the message of this book inspiring and thought-provoking. Hopefully, you can take some of the ideas with you on your journey to live a happier, healthier, and more fulfilling life.

I would very much appreciate you putting a review on Amazon, Google, or your favorite social media site. As an author relying on "word of mouth," your support is greatly appreciated. I would also like your feedback on the book. Feel free to send me your views, comments and how the book resonated with you. You can email me at **asingledayofpeace@gmail.com**

The Journey of Writing This Book

The idea of writing this book came to me many years ago, and it all started when I began questioning some of the principles of the Catholic Church. Raised Catholic, I attended Mass frequently. I did my best to instill this habit into my children. As my children entered their teenage years, they expressed a lack of a desire to participate in the weekly ritual. While partly excused as teenagers being typical teenagers, I couldn't ignore their perspective that they didn't feel inspired by the weekly event. They believed in God and Jesus Christ but didn't feel attending church did much for them.

I didn't want to persuade them with the argument my parents used, something like "because God wants you to go to church" (Catholic guilt). I encouraged them to see that going to church provided valuable lessons to integrate into their lives. Then, as the scandals became more public, like many, my children and I lost some faith in the leaders of the Catholic Church. My children would continue to attend Mass due to my ground rules, but they always left frustrated. They didn't leave inspired and didn't feel closer to God by attending. I eventually ceased my Sunday morning demands but, to this day, encourage them to speak to God daily in prayer. They tell me they do (but not every day!). As I grew more spiritual, I found myself questioning the "how" of the Catholic Church.

So, while I had the idea of this book for some time, I never got started. Then, as the story goes, one morning about six years ago, while jogging on the boardwalk along the ocean near my home, iPhone securely tucked into my pocket, I listened to an interview with Bruce Springsteen. The interviewer asked questions about writing songs, and Bruce said something that resonated with me. I'm paraphrasing, but he said, "Some people just have something to say and that is why they write. I have something to say, so I write songs."

When I heard that, I had to challenge myself because I, too, had something to say. But, for some reason, I never got around to saying it. Then, later that day, I read a quote by Dr. Wayne Dyer, the world-famous self-help author and public speaker, whose work I love. His quote: "Don't die with your music still inside you." Call it coincidence, serendipity, or the Universe sending me messages, but those two signals on the same day inspired me to finally get started.

Why the procrastination? First off, to be transparent, I wondered if anyone would really want to read what I had to say. Second, those that are kind enough to read my writing, well, they may not like the message so why risk the controversy? That said, I wanted to take the risk and go for it. As I thought about my decision to take the risk, I concluded that through this story I could possibly impact people in a positive way and give a little back.

So, I had an idea of creating a fictional story and used my religion as the theme to deliver a message, an opinion, a perspective. My intent is not to take a shot at the Catholic Church but to suggest that all religions can improve how they execute their mission, so that they are more effective at guiding their followers to be happy, healthy, and spiritual people.

I'm sure some readers will not agree with the perspectives shared. I'm sure some may be angry. On the other hand, I'm sure some will agree. And, there will be many in-between. Taking a phrase from the late Dr. Wayne Dyer, all I ask is… rather than outright disagreeing and biting off the end of my finger, take a moment to look where it is pointing.

ABOUT
KHARIS PUBLISHING

KHARIS PUBLISHING is an independent, traditional publishing house with a core mission to publish impactful books, and channel proceeds into establishing mini-libraries or resource centers for orphanages in developing countries, so these kids will learn to read, dream, and grow. Every time you purchase a book from Kharis Publishing or partner as an author, you are helping give these kids an amazing opportunity to read, dream, and grow. Kharis Publishing is an imprint of Kharis Media LLC. Learn more at
https://www.kharispublishing.com.

CPSIA information can be obtained
at www.ICGtesting.com
Printed in the USA
FSHW022302030621
82022FS